# The Bigg Boss

a Dubois Files mystery
by Joan H. Young

cover illustration by Linda J. Sandow
interior illustrations by Joan H. Young

To Jayden —
Joan H. Young

Published by Books Leaving Footprints
861 W US 10
Scottville, Michigan 49454

LCCN: 2018903764
ISBN: 1-948910-02-0
ISBN-13: 978-1-948910-02-6

# DUBOIS FILES BOOKS

# DEDICATION

To my grandmother, Emily M. Rowe, who
demonstrated in word and deed that the color of
a person's skin has nothing to do with the kind
of person they are.

# CORA'S INTRODUCTION

My name is Cora Caulfield, and I'm an older lady now. But when I was a child, my last name was Dubois. That's French, pronounced dew-BWAH. My friends and I had an exciting summer in 1953. It ended with breaking up a ring of thieves at the Cherry Pit Junction canning factory, where my father was the manager.

Jimmie, George and I were moving into the upper level classroom, leaving our friend Laszlo, and George's sister Ruby, in the other room. But on the very first day of school that September, someone began yelling at Ruby! Not everyone was happy that we had helped capture the robbers.

And then there was Mr. Bigg. He was the owner of the canning factory, and why he acted the way he did was certainly a mystery. I didn't think that was a riddle we could solve.

# BOOK FOUR – THE BIGG BOSS

# The East South River Road Neighborhood

1. Mosher
2. Szep
3. Dubois
4. Harris
5. Canning Factory
6. School
7. Store
8. R.R. Station
9. Migrant Housing

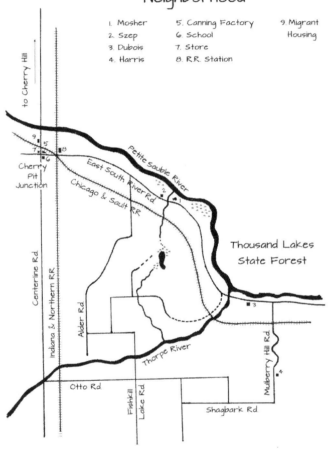

# 1. FIRST DAY OF SCHOOL

Tito Gonzales stood in the doorway of the lower elementary classroom with his arm outstretched. He was pointing straight at Ruby Harris, who was also starting second grade. His face was deep purple with some emotion, but it was hard to tell if he was going to be angry or if he was going to cry.

He did both. Tears began to run down his dark cheeks as he entered the room and yelled, "I saw you in the paper. You're part of that gang that put *Papá¹* in jail. *Te odio*!"²

Ruby's eyes got big and round, then narrowed to slits. She didn't understand the last words Tito had said, but it didn't sound like he wanted to be friends. She put her hands on her hips and

---

¹ say pah-PAH (or mah-MAH for Mamá). Father and Mother in Spanish
² say Tay OH-dee-oh. I hate you in Spanish.

said. "Your dad got himself in big trouble. We only helped catch him doing it."

But then Ruby started to cry too. She didn't like being yelled at. And being called part of a gang made her feel dirty, despite her clean hair and brand new dress and shoes. This was a rotten way to start the new school year.

Some of the other children of Mexican migrant workers grouped around Tito and started to chant, "Ruby's a cube, Ruby's a cube." She looked around for someone who would stick up for her but there wasn't anyone in sight who would help Ruby. Being called names wasn't new for her. It wasn't always easy being a Negro child when almost everyone else was white. At least a "cube" was only someone who wasn't popular, not anything worse. And she did have some good friends, although no one could really call them a gang.

Her older brother George, along with Cora Dubois and Jimmie Mosher, had all moved across the hall to the upper elementary room this September. They were now in fourth grade, and of the five friends, the ones Tito described as a gang, only Laszlo Szep and Ruby were left in Mrs. Bergman's room. Where was the teacher? The school bus had arrived early, but shouldn't the teacher have been there even earlier?

Just then, Laszlo came in the room. He didn't know exactly what was going on, but he saw the tears and heard the taunting voices. He dropped his lunch pail and new notebook on a desk and put his arm around Ruby's shoulders. He started yelling at Tito and his friends. Laszlo had been in Chicago with his mother and sisters when Tito's father was caught stealing from the Cherry Pit Junction canning factory, but everyone knew the story. It had been on the front page of the *Cherry Hill Herald* with a big picture of the four friends who broke up the real gang—the thieving employees who were stealing fruit and supplies and selling them. Tito's father, Juan Gonzales, drove the truck, and he was caught red-handed.[3]

---

[3] see *The ABZ Affair*

Footsteps clattered on the stairs--adults with leather soled shoes, not kids wearing sneakers. Mrs. Bergman and Miss Kelly hurried into the room. They must have been downstairs in the library or the all-purpose room. Except for restrooms and a janitor's closet, the square brick building had exactly four rooms—two classrooms upstairs and the other two rooms downstairs.

"What is going on here? Quiet down this instant!" Mrs. Bergman ordered in her sternest teacher voice. Everyone obeyed, and the room was suddenly so silent they could hear a bumblebee buzzing high up against a tall window.

Miss Kelly directed Tito and his friends to desks. "Sit down and be still."

At the same time, Mrs. Bergman took Ruby by the hand and led her to the front row of student desks. Ruby felt like she was the one being punished by being seated right in front of the teacher. The back of her neck was hot where she imagined Tito's angry eyes boring into her.

Laszlo sat down, too. Miss Kelly went across the hall and soon returned with all the fourth through sixth graders. They filed into the classroom and stood against the back wall in front of the world map. The uncomfortable silence continued while the teachers whispered to each other.

"All right," Mrs. Bergman began. "We would like to hear both sides of what this is all about. The new school year should be about making friends, not alienating others just because they look different."

Ruby wasn't sure what "alienating" meant, but it sounded bad, and she knew the problem wasn't about the color of anyone's skin.

The teacher continued. "Laszlo Szep," you will begin by explaining why you are yelling at children who are younger than you are.

Laszlo gulped. This was going to be his first full school year at the Cherry Pit Junction School. His family had come from Hungary in the early spring, and they now lived in the tenant house on the Mosher farm. He knew he'd be in big trouble at home if his parents were told he'd been in a fight at school. If it had been a fist fight, he would have won. Laszlo was strong. At least he spoke English well so he could explain; he'd learned how before they moved to the United States. He was starting third grade, the uppermost grade in this classroom, and he was supposed to be a good example to the others. He began, "Those kids were making fun of my friend, Ruby," he said. "I didn't like the name they were calling her, so I did yell at them. I'm sorry I yelled, but I'm not sorry I stuck up for Ruby."

"Tito, why were you and your friends calling Ruby names? Don't deny it, Miss Kelly and I heard you," Mrs. Bergman said.

Tito was Mexican. He was brown-skinned and wiry and spoke both Spanish and English. He had been in lots of schools and lots of scrapes in his short life, and he wasn't intimidated by adults, even teachers. He thought he'd probably move soon anyway. Migrant workers never stayed in one place very long. Because he'd never finished a school year he was actually old enough to be in third grade.

He stuck out his chin and said loudly, "She and her friends are the ones who put my father in jail. I was telling her I did not like it."

In the back of the room, a boy raised his hand and called, "Mrs. Bergman, may I say something." It was Jimmie Mosher, the oldest of the five friends.

## 2. TITO'S SAD STORY

Mrs. Bergman was clearly in charge in this room. "You may not speak, Jimmie. Not yet. I want to hear from Tito."

Jimmie sighed. He had only wanted to explain that Ruby didn't put Juan Gonzales in jail, but then he realized the teachers must know that.

"Tito Gonzales, come up here."

Tito liked the attention, even if he was probably going to be punished for something. To be standing in front gave him credibility as a leader with his friends, and all the migrant boys and girls who had been harassing Ruby now turned their eyes on the skinny but tough second-grader. The Mexican families' lives were hard and they stuck together.

Tito hurried to stand beside the teacher and began, "*Papá* was taken away to jail just a week ago, and it is very bad at home without him. They need to let him out so he can come home and help us."

"How are things bad at home?" Mrs. Bergman asked.

"*Mamá* is all alone to get the work done. She has to go to the factory every day but there is no one who can watch the babies. All the other women also have to work, and now that school has started those of us who are old enough to help, but not old enough to work all day in the orchard, aren't there to babysit. We can't afford to lose the money if my mother stays home."

Miss Kelly wanted to know how many babies were at the Gonzales house.

Tito's chest swelled with pride. "I am the oldest. I am not a baby, and my name is Tito Fernando Gonzales, which means a bold titan. That is like a giant. Now I must be man of the house. I have a sister who is two. Her name is Francesca Guadelupe Gonzales. Marco Ángel is the smallest. He is not even a year old. There was another, between me and Francesca. Her name was Esma Felicita, but she died."

Ruby thought it would be very sad to have a sister die. She knew that children died of polio and scarlet fever, and in accidents, but she had never known any of them personally.

"But, someone must be watching the little ones while your mother works." Mrs. Bergman said.

"There is an old grandmother, *la vieja*,[4] who does not hear and can not walk. Her heart is too weak to work in the factory, and she will go back to Mexico soon, but *Mamá* takes the little ones to her in the morning and I will get them after school and take them home. Francesca will have to stay in a playpen all day because Senora Elena, the old one, can not chase her around. How can she take care of babies? She can not even change their diapers!" Tito pounded his fist on a desk to emphasize how upset he was.

"I can see that you are really frustrated," said Mrs. Bergman. "But these things aren't Ruby's

---

[4] say lah vee-A-uh. Spanish for an older respected woman

fault, or her friends' fault. Your father did something very wrong. You understand that, don't you, Tito?"

"He could not help it!" the boy exclaimed.

Miss Kelly spoke up. "Certainly he could. We each have to choose between doing what is right and wrong. Stealing from your employer is a very bad thing, and it's a crime. Perhaps if your father pleads guilty he'll receive a lighter sentence."

"He only wanted to help our family." Tito was shouting again. "We had decided to stay here for the winter so I could go to just this one school to learn more, instead of moving so often. But the windows are cracked in our house and there is no heat. *Papá* was going to buy a wood stove, and some furniture that isn't broken. We all sleep on the floor except for the babies who sleep in the playpen. The man who owns the building is a bad man. He won't fix things. *Papá* wants to make our lives better. Why is that wrong?"

"What your father wants for your family is honorable, Tito, but he tried to accomplish it in the wrong ways," Mrs. Bergman said. "Do you understand the difference?"

Tito hung his head. "I guess so, Teacher. But what are we supposed to do? The canning factory will close for the winter in October, and who will give a 'dirty Mexican' a job?"

# 3. WHAT CAN WE DO?

Cora and Ruby were sitting in the Dubois living room, talking. The boys were making toast with jelly in the kitchen. The friends had all gotten off the school bus at Cora's house so they could have a meeting. The bus driver simply told them to be sure to call their parents. Everyone knew everyone else's family, and looked out for one another.

The first day of school was over. Tito and Laszlo both had to stay inside at recess as punishment for yelling at other students. But after those exciting first few minutes of the day things had calmed down and settled into the expected routine of being assigned seats; passing out textbooks; writing essays and then reading them out loud; trying to remember how to use math skills; and making yellow, red, and orange construction paper leaves for the bulletin boards.

"My reading book is called *Friends and Neighbors*," Ruby said. "But it's too easy. I could already read it last year. What's yours?"

"Fourth graders get *Times and Places*," Cora answered. It's all right, but the stories are short. I'm glad each class had library time today so we could take out longer books to bring home. I got three."

"Look what I bought with some of the money from the job your father gave us," Ruby said. From her new three-ring binder she pulled a colorful folder made of lightweight cardboard. "Paper dolls! Will you help me punch them out so I don't break the tabs?"

Cora sighed. She didn't care much about paper dolls, but she did care a lot about Ruby. "Sure," she answered.

Just then, Laszlo called from the kitchen, "There's a pile of toast ready. Cora's mom says we should eat in here."

They gathered around the kitchen table. There were only four chairs, and since Ruby was the smallest, she sat on the stool that had pull-down steps so it could also be a short ladder to reach high shelves. The smell of the warm bread and homemade peach jam was comforting. Mrs. Dubois had poured glasses of cold milk and it went perfectly with the sweet fruit and crunchy toast. She smiled at the children and went to the back yard to take laundry off the clothesline.

Jimmie was the tallest and oldest of the friends, and that made him the natural leader. When they were full, he licked his fingers and began, "We need to talk about what Tito said in school today."

"Yeah, I'm not a cube," Ruby said.

Her brother George responded, "A cube isn't so bad. We've been called lots worse things. Sometimes doing the right thing makes people upset."

"Sticks and stones may break my bones, but words can never hurt me," Cora quoted in a sing-song voice.

"That's only partly true," Laszlo said. "Words don't break bones, but they can hurt you inside. My parents got called 'Hunkies' and 'Bohunks' when we first got off the ship in New York. I could tell it made them sad. No one asked our names; people shoved us around and assumed we were stupid. We smelled bad because there weren't showers in our part of the ship. People called us dirty and thought we all planned to mine coal somewhere in Pennsylvania.

"Like when Tito said people wouldn't give a 'dirty Mexican' a job," Ruby said. "But Cora's dad would have helped him find a winter job if he had been honest."

Cora's father was the manager at the Cherry Pit Junction canning factory. "That's right," Cora agreed. "After all, Mr. Gonzales had been picked to be night watchman, so he must have been doing good work before that."

"That's why I wanted to meet at Cora's house," Jimmie explained. Maybe Mr. Dubois can tell us why Tito's father might have gone wrong. He also knows the owner of the factory."

"Why is that important?" Ruby asked.

"Because he also owns the buildings Tito and his friends live in."

"Mr. Bigg? The one who gave us money to start a college savings account?" Laszlo asked. He was surprised.

George was thinking. He said, "So Mr. Bigg was willing to give us money for helping him, and he spends money for new equipment and repairs at the factory, but he won't pay to clean up and fix the houses for the employees. That seems strange."

"Maybe Tito was making some of that up to make us feel sorry for him," Cora said. "We can find out. Let's go visit them on Saturday. We could offer to watch the little ones for a while, or help Mrs. Gonzales do some housework."

"Hmm, I'm not crazy about washing dishes. But maybe we can fix something," George offered.

"What are you going to fix?" Mr. DuBois' deep voice broke in on their conversation. He was just entering through the back door with his briefcase in one hand. He removed his hat and jokingly placed it on George's head where it slipped down over the boy's eyes. Everyone laughed.

Cora ran to hug her father. She took the car keys from him and hung them on a rack beside the door. Then she pulled the hat off George's head. "Your head isn't big enough to be the big boss yet."

"Hey, that's who Mr. Bigg is," George said. "He's the B-I-G-G boss."

Mr. Dubois scratched his head. "OK, now I'm really perplexed. You kids are going to fix something that has to do with the owner of the factory?"

"Is it true he owns the building where the Mexicans live?" Laszlo asked.

"Yes, that's right," Cora's father said.

The children asked a lot of questions about what Mr. Bigg was like, but they didn't get answers that satisfied them. Mr. Dubois explained that the boss lived in Cold Rapids, a big city downstate. He owned many businesses, worked in a large office building, and rarely came to Forest County. He controlled the money and made decisions about how it was spent. Cora's father wasn't sure, but he thought Mr. Bigg hadn't visited the Cherry Pit Junction canning factory for at least five years.

Ruby was getting bored. She tugged on Cora's hand. "Come help me with the paper dolls now."

The boys ran out into the back yard to play catch, and the girls went back to the living room.

## 4. PAPER DOLLS ARE SILLY

Cora settled down on the floor beside Ruby, although she didn't think dolls and clothes were much fun. The punch-out book she wanted had a cardboard model of Captain Hook's pirate ship from the Peter Pan movie, which had finally come to the Starlight Theater in Cherry Hill. Her parents had taken her to see it only a few days ago, and she was dreaming of Peter, Tinkerbell, Tiger Lily, and the crocodile.

Some of the pages in Ruby's book were lightweight cardboard. They were printed in color on both sides and the edges of the dolls were perforated. On those pages were four different children who were wearing nothing but their underwear! Their clothing was on separate paper pages, and there were tabs you could fold around the bodies to make the clothes stay on the dolls.

Carefully the girls pushed the cutouts from the background until there were two boys and two girl dolls who needed outfits. Only one arm ended up with a small tear.

"I wish there was a little dark girl, like me," Ruby said.

Cora thought about that. "I wonder why books always have white children, and baby dolls are always white."

"I looked at all the pictures in the reading book at school and there aren't any kids with black fuzzy hair like mine. There aren't even any boys as dark as Tito and his friends," Ruby said sadly. "It's like we aren't even there. And now Tito is mad at me."

"Tito doesn't know what he's saying. He's just upset that his father isn't home. We'll find out more on Saturday," Cora said.

The girls punched out some of the clothes for the dolls and folded the tabs so the shirts and dresses hung on the girl's shoulders. It was harder to keep the pants on the boy dolls.

"Get your crayons, Ruby," Cora said, suddenly getting an idea. When Ruby gave her a funny look, she added, "I won't break any; I promise."

"OK," Ruby said, and ran to her room.

When she came back she was carrying a shoebox filled with pencils, scissors, a ruler, old broken crayon stubs, and her new, treasured box of forty-eight Crayola crayons. She set it down and pulled one from the packet. "Did you already know about this color in the big box?"

"What are you talking about?" Cora asked.

"See this?"

Cora took the peachy crayon from her friend.

"Look at the name of the color," Ruby instructed.

Cora turned the crayon sideways and read, "'Flesh.' Oh, I see what you mean. This isn't the right color for you or George or Tito. Not everyone's skin is this color."

"I think I'm more like Raw Umber if I don't press hard," Ruby said.

"Then let's use that color and make one of these dolls like you," Cora said. "We can make her hair black and put curls in the pigtails to be like yours."

Ruby wasn't sure. "Is it all right to color over what was printed?"

"It's your book, and you bought it with your own money. Of course it's OK."

"We can even make clothes you like. Get some plain paper," Cora said. This was going to be more fun than punching things out of a book.

Ruby left again, and returned with some paper that was blank on one side. "I took some of George's scrap paper, but he won't mind. He saves it all the time."

"Good. Now trace around the doll shape with a pencil. Real lightly," Cora said. "Draw the shape of your first-day-of-school dress. Make the puffed sleeves around the arm, and make it stick out beside the legs, like a skirt does. Now color it bright yellow, but leave the collar white."

Ruby followed her friend's lead, copying the dress she was still wearing.

"Now draw on tabs, just like the ones from the book."

"I get it," Ruby said with a smile. "Now I'll use the scissors."[5]

Soon the friends had a paper boy and girl who looked very much like George and Ruby, and were wearing the same color clothes as the real brother and sister.

Out in the back yard, the boys were playing with a soft rubber ball. They had invented a game. They took turns throwing the ball onto the roof of the house and then trying to catch it. The first time it had to be caught without a bounce. The second time the ball had to bounce only once on the ground and then caught. Then, two bounces and so on. If they missed, they had to start over. Every time the ball hit the lawn it would go off at some crazy angle. So far, Laszlo was the only one who had caught a ball after two bounces, but he hadn't been able to increase

---

[5] see instructions to make paper dolls at the end of the book

that to three. The ball either went wild or lost too much energy and turned into a grounder after the second bounce.

"Boys," Cora's father called. "I'll take you home if you come now. That way you won't have to walk."

"That would be great! It's only a couple miles, but I'd appreciate it." Jimmie said. "Thank you, Mr. Dubois."

Jimmie, George and Laszlo came in the house and found the girls drawing more dresses, shirts and pants.

"What are you doing?" Laszlo asked.

"Playing paper dolls," Ruby said.

"Dolls are silly," Laszlo replied without thinking that he might hurt his friends' feelings.

Ruby held up the two dark dolls with black curly hair. "No they're not. We made some just like George and me."

# 5. CHERRY PITS AND CINDER BLOCKS

The first week of school was both exciting and depressing. It was difficult to spend most of the day inside when the sun was bright and the grass was still green. But new books and supplies, new skills, new clothes, and new activities made it more tolerable.

The friends agreed to meet at Jimmie's house just after lunch on Saturday. Each had spent the morning doing weekly household chores. For the afternoon they would go see where Tito lived. George, Ruby and Cora pedaled into the Mosher yard together, and now that Laszlo had a bicycle of his own he could go along on all the adventures.

Cora's mother had helped her bake an apple pie to take as a gift. It was wrapped in a clean towel and safely snuggled into Cora's bike basket.

"Tito's family sees apples all day long," Jimmie had said earlier in the week. "They won't want any more apples."

But Cora argued that even though that was true, probably no one had any time to make something special like a pie.

Laszlo's little sister, Eniko, had outgrown some of her toys, and Mrs. Szep said they should share with Tito's family. They chose a dog pull-toy to take to Francesca. It was harder to decide what to give baby Marco. Finally they picked out a soft doll Mrs. Szep had made when Eniko was much younger. It was brown and shaped like a gingerbread man. There was rick-rack around the edges that looked like frosting, and it had two black buttons for eyes.

"Shouldn't we take something for Tito?" George asked.

Ruby frowned. "Why? He wasn't nice to us."

"That's the whole point," Cora said. "He wasn't nice because something bad happened to his family and he was upset. We know it's not our fault, so we shouldn't punish Tito just because he's confused."

"Let's offer something. If he doesn't want it, I'm sure he'll tell us," Jimmie said.

But they couldn't figure out what would be a good gift.

"Wait! I know," Ruby exclaimed. "He doesn't have the school supplies he's supposed to. He was borrowing from his friends all week and making everyone angry."

"I have an extra ruler," Laszlo said.

"I'll give him my crayons," Jimmie offered. "I can get another box. And I have an extra pencil too."

Since Laszlo's house was very near Jimmie's, it only took a few minutes for them to collect these items.

"What about paper?" George asked.

They all stared at each other, but second-graders were supposed to have the paper with really wide spaces between the lines, and neither Jimmie nor Laszlo had any. Ruby was the only one young enough to still use this kind, and her house was too far away to ride back and get some today.

Also, Ruby wasn't feeling particularly friendly toward Tito. Although she had liked the idea of giving the boy something, she wasn't as excited about it when she was asked to give up something of hers.

"C'mon, Ruby. Tito is even poorer than we are," George said. "At least our dad has work all year since Mr. Dubois said he could use him on the winter maintenance crew. We don't have to move all the time, either."

Ruby reluctantly agreed to add a note saying she would give Tito some paper on Monday. Jimmie ran into his house again and got a brown grocery bag to hold the items and a scratch pad sheet on which Ruby could write her promise of paper.

Finally they were ready to go. It had taken longer to prepare than it did to ride the two-and-a-half miles to Cherry Pit Junction.

This tiny crossroads wasn't really a town. It was the junction of two railroad lines, the Indiana & Northern which ran north-south, and the east-west Chicago-Sault line. There was a railroad station with one siding, and a small store. The elementary school the children attended was also located there, just to the south of where East South River Road met Centerline Road. That crossroad was the exact center of Forest County.

In the triangle between the two tracks and East South River Road was the canning factory. This was the business Cora's father managed, and the place where the migrants worked. The name came from the huge mounds of cherry pits that were dumped to the south of the school building every summer. The piles were so big they were actually small hills.

Laszlo had only lived in the United States for five months. "I don't really understand what 'migrants' are," he said as they pedaled their bikes.

Jimmie answered, "Most of the migrants come north from Mexico in the spring. They do the hard, hot farm work, like picking asparagus. This isn't the only house. Lots of the farmers have their own buildings."

Cora interrupted, "'Migrant' just means 'people on the move.'" She liked to make sure everyone understood the meanings of words.

"We helped pick asparagus one Saturday this spring," George said. "It really hurts your back to lean over all day."

Jimmie continued, "They also hoe out the weeds—whole fields of cucumbers or squash, and then they harvest vegetables and fruit right through till fall.

"It never ends," Cora said. "Strawberries, cherries, blueberries, peaches, apricots, and apples."

Ruby didn't want to be the only one with no information to contribute. She remembered that the Mexican children usually started school in the fall and then disappeared. "They go home where it's warm for the winter, or maybe to places where vegetables grow all year," she guessed correctly.

"I see them working outside in the hot sun, the rain, or even when it's really cold," Jimmie said. "They can't wait, like I can, to tend the garden until better weather, because there's too much to do. There are acres and acres of plants."

"But some of them work inside the canning factory," Laszlo pointed out.

Cora knew the factory best because of her father's job. "Most of the women do, and some of the men run the big machines. Kids can't work there 'til they're fourteen. There's a law. But they can work in the fields."

"Lots of them don't speak English," Ruby said. "When we started first grade last year, Tito couldn't understand hardly anything the teacher said. But he sure seems to have learned a lot in the last year. I wonder if his mother will be able to understand us."

"Thanks," Laszlo said. "I get it, now. Our family is staying in the Mosher tenant house and trying to fit in. The migrants just move together from place to place and don't have to make new friends."

They rode into Cherry Pit Junction toward the factory's migrant housing. It was a long single-story structure built of cinder blocks that looked like a run-down motel. There were about ten doors in the front, and each one had a single window beside it. The roof sloped toward the back. Blotchy pale green paint was chipping from the concrete, and there was no grass around the housing, only bare dirt.

The dry dust swirled up as Jimmie and his friends braked their bikes. Unfamiliar music blared through an open window, but the beat was lively. Ruby liked it. It made her want to dance.

Cora sneezed. "Which one is Tito's place?"

## 6. WHERE TITO LIVES

Four little barefoot children ran toward the bikes. "*Quiénes son?*"[6] they asked.

Ruby recognized the oldest girl from school, although she was only a first-grader. "Speak English, Juanita. Tell us where Tito lives." she commanded.

Juanita said nothing, but pointed to the last door in the green building. The other children gathered in close, giggling and touching the bicycles. One little boy pushed the lever on Cora's bell, making it ding over and over again.

"What are we going to do?" Cora asked. "What if they try to ride our bikes?"

"I don't think we can stop them unless one of us stands guard," Jimmie said.

George knocked on the door Juanita had pointed out. A tired-looking woman opened it

---

[6] say KEY-en-nays sewn. Who are you? in Spanish

and stuck her head outside. She looked around. "You are friends of my Tito, *si,* yes?" She asked. Then she looked at the small children. "*Fuera!* Go home," she ordered. With many giggles, the younger boys and girls vanished.

"Thank you," Cora said as she lifted the towel-wrapped pie from her bicycle basket. "May we come in? We brought something for you."

"*Pásate,* Come inside. Tito, *aquí!*" she said, turning her head and calling for Tito to come.

The woman stepped back and the children entered the room. It was chilly and the light was dim. There was a table and several chairs. Two narrow mattresses were stacked against the wall and a little girl sat on top of them playing with a baby. Tito appeared in the doorway from a room at the rear of the apartment.

Cora placed the pie on the table and removed the covering. "It's an apple pie," she said. "We hope you like it."

"What is pie?" Mrs. Gonzales asked, looking at the round dessert with its golden crust.

Cora and Jimmie looked at each other, then Jimmie spoke up. "It has a crust made with flour and shortening. You put fruit and sugar, and spices, inside and another crust on top and bake it. Cora made this one for you herself."

"Well, my mom helped me with the crust. Crust is tricky," Cora said humbly.

"It's sort of like an *empanadilla,*[7] *Mamá*," Tito said. "Sometimes the white kids at school have pie in their lunches." His words didn't sound angry, but he was scowling.

"And we brought toys for Francesca and Marco," Ruby said. She held out the paper sack.

Francesca heard her name and came running. Ruby took out the wiggly dog and showed the little girl how to pull it with the string.

Baby Marco was old enough to understand that there were interesting things happening and he wasn't involved. He began to howl. Laszlo grabbed the gingerbread man doll and

---

[7] say em-PAHN-uh-dee-ya. Spanish for a tortilla with filling, folded and baked or fried.

took it to Marco who squeezed it happily and stuck one of the feet in his mouth.

Tito still looked unhappy. "Why are you bringing gifts to my family?" He asked. "Because you think this will make me like you?"

Cora ignored his rude comment. "We have some things for you too, Tito," she said. "Things you need for school." She spread the supplies on the table.

"Thank you, *Gracias!*" Mrs. Gonzales exclaimed. "We need such things, but could not afford them."

Tito began speaking angrily to his mother, but the children couldn't understand the words.

She answered him in another fast flurry of Spanish. It was clear enough from her tone of voice that she did not like Tito's attitude.

The boy sulked, but did not argue back.

"Sit down, children," Mrs. Gonzales said. "We will eat your pie."

"But it's for you," Jimmie protested.

"*No importa*; it is not important," the woman said. "We share. And I have no refrigerator to keep food for long."

"No refrigerator?" Cora asked, looking around. "How can you make meals without a refrigerator?"

"We eat what I cook, right away, so it can not spoil. We have a stove."

Jimmie focused on the main reason why they had come to visit. "We'd like to see your house, if you'll let us. Tito said you want to live here this winter, but there's no heat. Is that true? How will you stay warm?"

"I do not know what we will do. Perhaps we can buy a kerosene heater at the hardware store if I can save enough money. The fruit season is almost over, and I have no job after that."

Cora remembered the smell of the kerosene heater at her grandmother's. She thought it would be awful to live with that all winter.

"Show them the house, *Mamá*," Tito said bitterly. "Cora's father is the boss, but he will do nothing, you'll see."

Cora felt a twinge of anger shoot through her, but she held her tongue.

"That's not quite true," Jimmie explained. "The factory is owned by a Mr. Bigg who lives in Cold Rapids. He's the one who decides what gets done with the buildings. We'd like to ask him to fix things, but we have to know what to ask for."

*"Si, si,"* Tito's mother said, pointing upward at a bare unlit light bulb hanging from a wire in the ceiling. "This electric light, she is broken. We have no lamp in this room after dark."

She hustled the children into the kitchen which was a smaller room across the back of the block apartment. "This is the stove. The oven does not work, but there is always gas, so we can make tortillas. And there is safe water in the sink. These are the good things."

A large white sink was attached to the wall. Rust stains streamed down beneath the faucet which dripped continuously. Curtains made of burlap sacks hung at the window. The light bulb in the kitchen worked, although it also dangled from a bare wire. Cupboards with no doors covered one wall of the room, and they held dishes, pans, some canned goods, and bags of dry beans and cornmeal. Potato crates had been arranged around a small table with a stick jammed under one corner where it was missing a leg.

"The children eat here," she explained. "You can see for yourself that both this window and the one in front are cracked. Even if I get a heater, the drafts they will come in."

"Where's the bathroom?" Ruby asked.

"There is a toilet at the other end of the row of houses, and one shower all the workers use. If we are the only family here in the winter that will not be so bad. Is not so good in the summer when everyone comes in dirty from the fields."

"Wow," Jimmie couldn't think of much to say.

"Do you think this Mr. Bigg will listen to you?" Rosa Gonzales asked.

"I sure hope so," Cora said.

"We will share your apple pie and say a prayer to Saint Jude," she said, reaching for a stack of mismatched plates. "Tito, please get the forks."

## 7. DEAR MR. BIGG

"How can we make Mr. Bigg listen to us?" Cora asked her father that evening.

"I'm not sure," Philippe Dubois admitted. "I've told him several times that the housing is sub-standard, and he's going to have a harder and harder time getting workers to commit to the factory. Some of the orchard owners have cleaned up their buildings, and now people go to those farms first. Families want a decent place to stay, no matter where they come from."

"Why would anyone live in a place like Tito's house, Papa?"

"They still earn more money in the factory than they do in the fields. None of the migrant housing is really nice, but some of it is at least in good repair," her father answered.

"Mr. Bigg is a mystery. But I'm not sure he is one we can solve," Cora said, shaking her head.

***

After church and dinner on Sunday, Cora put on her favorite blue shirt and a pair of denim overalls. These were the only kinds of clothes she really liked to wear. Church dresses were especially itchy and bothersome, and although school dresses were more comfortable they were still... well... dresses. She was annoyed at how unfair life sometimes seemed. Girls had to wear dresses, just because they were girls. The crayon company didn't seem to know dark skin existed. Families like Tito's were treated badly just because they were different. She thought maybe a bicycle ride would take her mind off these puzzles.

As she rode out of her yard, George and Ruby yelled from the corner of Mulberry Hill Road. They pedaled hard to catch up.

"Where are you going?" George asked.

"Where are you going?" Cora asked.

"Nowhere much," George said.

"Me, too," Cora agreed.

"Let's go find Jimmie and Laszlo," Ruby suggested. "We can go nowhere together."

Half an hour later the five friends were sitting in their underground hideout, the old cellar they had discovered early in the summer. They were discussing Mr. Bigg.

"How can we make a grownup we don't even know change his mind?" Ruby asked.

"He's a businessman," Jimmie said, thinking out loud. "He probably likes things done in a certain way. Maybe we should write him a letter."

"Maybe we should each write a letter. Five letters would impress him more than one," George said.

Cora jumped up from the keg she had been sitting on. "I know! We'll ask the teachers if both classes at school can write letters. All those letters will get his attention."

\*\*\*

The teachers agreed. "We'll do a lesson on the proper way to write a business letter," Miss Kelley said.

Mrs. Bergman was especially pleased. She thought it would be much more meaningful than copying a sample letter out of a workbook.

"Now tell us about where Tito lives, so we can plan what should be put in a letter."

When the children explained the condition of the migrant housing, the teachers were shocked.

"This is an important cause," Mrs. Bergman said.

"We'll do it this week," Miss Kelly added. She looked grim.

***

On Thursday morning, after attendance and the Pledge of Allegiance, everyone filed downstairs and sat at the lunch tables in the large multi-purpose room, which was the only space where the entire school could easily meet together. The teachers explained the project and that the upper grades would write longer letters, in cursive. The lower grades would print a shorter amount of text. Everyone was told to use their best penmanship, because this was not just an exercise. Tito's family, and others who lived in the canning factory housing, were counting on them.

On a portable blackboard Miss Kelly had written the list of things that needed fixing at the migrant apartments. "We've brought the classes together, because we want you to think about why these things will be a problem for the Gonzales family this winter," she said.

Javier's hand went up immediately. He was in fifth grade. "The rest of us are leaving in a few weeks. But with no electric light, that boy Tito can't see to read his books this winter. What good will his ed-u-ca-tion do then?" He said "education" with a sneer.

"You have a good point," Mrs. Bergman said, writing it on the blackboard. "About the lights. But you should be happy for Tito. Perhaps you'll be staying in school next year."

"I like Mexico," Javier said. He pronounced it MEH-he-ko. but he did not talk back after that.

Soon, the list also included these items:

Tito's family will get sick this winter without any heat.

Broken windows are not safe and won't keep out the cold.

It's not nice to have to walk outside to a different room to go to the bathroom.

The dripping faucet wastes water.

Without an oven Mrs. Gonzales can't bake food like chicken or cakes.

Rats and mice can get in the open shelves and eat their food.

Mrs. Gonzales won't sleep well without a bed, so she will fall asleep at work and get in trouble.

The format for the letters was already printed on a second chalkboard. Everyone copied those parts.

"You must each pick just one or two problems to point out to Mr. Bigg. In your second paragraph, suggest what he should do to fix the problem," Miss Kelly explained to Jimmie's class. "Don't just complain, come up with solutions. Then add a closing, and sign your name."

By lunchtime there were forty-three letters ready to be put into a large brown envelope.


Here is the text of the letter Jimmie wrote:

Cherry Pit Junction School
Cherry Hill, Michigan
September 17, 1953

Mr. Harold L. Bigg
Bigg, Inc.
374 10th Avenue
Cold Rapids, Michigan

Dear Mr. Bigg:

Some of my friends and I visited the building you own where Tito Gonzales lives. It needs a lot of work to be healthy for anyone to live there. His mother, Rosa, works in the canning factory, and they are going to stay all winter so Tito can go to school and get an education. No one can live here in the winter without heat, and even if they buy a space heater, the broken windows will just let all the heat out. The baby might get sick.

Please replace the broken windows and give the Gonzales family a warm place to stay.

Sincerely yours,
James Mosher

## 8. WAITING AND WONDERING

The children did not know it, but included with their carefully written or printed letters were two much longer ones, typed. These were from Mrs. Bergman and Miss Kelly. The teachers had been shocked at the living conditions in the migrant housing and were eager to tell Mr. Harold L. Bigg their thoughts.

Friday morning, the teachers announced that the package of letters had been mailed. "Mr. Bigg will probably receive them on Monday. We should expect an answer on Thursday or Friday," Mrs. Bergman said.

But the next Friday came and went with no mail, and so the earliest a letter might come from Cold Rapids was Monday the 28th of September. The month was almost over, and October might be nice, or it might be wet and chilly—not good weather for doing repairs.

\*\*\*

Ruby skidded her bike into the damp grass of Jimmie's lawn and fell over sideways. "Hey, look what I made!" she yelled, picking herself up and pulling some papers from the lumpy bag stuffed into her wire bike basket.

"We aren't going to wait for Mr. Bigg," Cora announced. She dismounted from her bicycle more cautiously, and George was right behind her. Cora also had a sack full of something in her basket, and there was a cardboard box tied onto George's rear carrier with twine.

"What's in the packages?" Laszlo asked, wiping his mouth and coming off the porch to meet them with half an apple still in his hand. Jimmie stepped down, too. The boys had been resting after Saturday lunch. They'd spent the morning sorting apples, choosing the best and largest ones which could be sold in town. The rest would go to the canning factory.

"We asked our parents if there were clothes we could give the Mexican families. They helped us clean out closets, and I've got towels and curtains, too. Even a blanket," Cora said.

Ruby was still holding something in her hand. She shook the papers for emphasis. "But look what else I did. I made flyers to hand out at church tomorrow. Cora made some too. With all of us, we go to three different churches."

"So what?" Laszlo asked.

"So, adults might have real things they don't need. Maybe a stove that works, or beds stored in a barn."

"A table that isn't broken," George added.

Cora said, "We can hand these papers out tomorrow and see if we can get some big stuff."

"And somebody with a truck to move it all," Ruby said.

"My dad might do that," Laszlo said.

"We'll need more flyers," Jimmie said. His eyes were bright. "This is a good idea, Ruby."

The children hauled the bundled clothing and household items onto Jimmie's porch. "They'll be OK there," he said. "Let's make a lot more papers to hand out."

\*\*\*

Sunday afternoon, two trucks pulled up in front of the green building where Tito's family hoped to live all winter. Javier, Juanita and other children, along with their parents, were still living there, but would leave for the South when the apple processing was finished at the canning factory.

Visitors in trucks were exciting. In seconds, the vehicles were surrounded by curious residents. In minutes, brown men were shaking hands with black and white men, and the trucks were unloaded.

Several cars pulled in. Women from the Baptist church in Cherry Hill stepped from one, and Catholics from the other, carrying casserole dishes. Another car arrived. It was full of laughing Negro ladies from the American Methodist Episcopal church in Emily City. They stopped laughing and started singing in harmony, "Nobody knows the trouble I've seen, nobody knows but Jesus."

Tito's little sister, Francesca, began dancing around the ladies with the wide smiles and beautiful voices.

The men assembled bed frames and hauled chairs and tables into the shabby rooms. Mrs. Gonzales' old stove came out of her kitchen and a newer one, with a working oven, was hooked up to the gas.

When almost everything was moved, an old man, who spoke only Spanish, brought out a guitar and strummed some notes. Quickly he shifted into a fast-paced song and the young men and boys began to dance.

Next, the A.M.E. ladies sang, "Ev'ry time I feel the Spirit moving in my heart I will pray..."

The old man smiled a toothless grin and began playing "La Cucaracha," faster and faster, and all the children spun in circles until they were rolling on the ground.

The day was turning out to be wonderful, almost like a party. One table had been left outside. It was now covered with dishes of food. Everyone was filling paper plates and hugging each other with no regard to the color of skin or language.

Everyone except Tito. He stood off to the side looking wary. Francesca tried to pull him toward the others and he pushed her away. She ran to her mother, crying.

And looming in Jimmie's thoughts was the huge question, "Would Mr. Bigg actually fix any of the serious problems with the building?"

## 9. WHAT TITO FOUND

After all the food had been eaten and the visitors had left, Tito's mother, Rosa Gonzales, took him to task. They spoke in Spanish, because it was their native tongue. "Tito, why are you still so angry with your friends?" she asked.

"They are not my friends. They think they can make me like them by giving us things they would have thrown away."

Rosa held Tito by the shoulders and scolded, "These are good clothes they have given us, a stove that works right, and two beds to get us all off the cold floor. You should appreciate it when people are kind to us. We need this help."

"Because they put *Papá* in jail, they feel guilty. They are doing this for themselves, to cover for their mistake."

"Tito Fernando, your father is the one who made the mistake, and he will pay for that. Your heart is dark tonight. When you go to bed you must pray for a heart *lleno de luz*, filled with light," Rosa said with a sigh.

Tito turned away in anger and walked into his house. He was thirsty and went to the kitchen to get a glass of water. As he crossed in front of the "new" stove he noticed that the men must have bumped the corner of the cupboard. The entire side was pulled slightly away from the back wall. He was about to go get his mother and add this to his complaints about the gifts when he saw something else.

Sticking out from behind the wood at the broken corner was a pink envelope. He grabbed the paper and tugged. Another envelope came into view and then another. Tito got a table knife and used it to pry the wood away from the wall. Behind the cupboard was a whole pile of letters. He dropped the knife and stuck the envelopes in the back of his pants, under his shirt.

Then he got his drink and went outside to find a private place to examine this discovery. He wandered across the road and sat on a stump at the back side of the little store. It was closed on Sundays, so no one was likely to see him there.

He took out the envelopes and counted them. There were six, all pink. Not a single one had a name or address on the outside, but they were sealed. Tito thought about this. He knew they didn't belong to him, but how could he figure out who they did belong to if he couldn't open at least one? He couldn't.

Tito chose an envelope that must have gotten damp. The glue that held it together was failing, and by working at it carefully he lifted one of the flaps without tearing it. The paper inside was also pink with words written in blue ink.

"*Caramba*," Tito said softly. "They are in cursive. I can't read these letters."[8]

---

[8] see instructions to learn cursive writing at the end of the book

But then he discovered he could read some things. There was a date at the top that was all numbers. "The fourteenth of May, 1930," he read. "That was a long time ago."

Because the school at Cherry Pit Junction had several grades together in each of the two classrooms, often younger students who were bright learned skills early. There was a chart of cursive letters all around the top of the room. Tito knew some of them. He studied the beginning of the letter, and decided it said, "Dearest Harry." The ending wasn't too hard either. "I love you," was easy to guess, but the signature was harder. Tito spelled it out, letter by letter. "K-i-t-t-y P-e-r-h-a-m." A girl named Kitty? But she would be a grownup now, older than his mother.

Tito pondered how he could use the letters to tease someone or get something he wanted. Not once did he remember that his first thought had been to find the owner and return them.

It was starting to get dark and he heard his mother calling. Tito pushed the letters under his shirt once more and walked toward home. He'd be sharing the new bed with Francesca. Just for a moment he forgot to be angry and thought how nice it would be to have sheets and a pillow and to not sleep on a dirty mattress on the floor.

## 10. DEAR CHILDREN

Monday morning, the third week of the school year, lessons were becoming routine. But not this morning. There was a letter in the mail from Bigg, Inc.. The postman walked it up to Miss Kelly's classroom instead of just placing it in the rural mailbox by the road. It seemed that everyone had heard what the children were trying to accomplish.

Miss Kelly walked across the hall and got Mrs. Bergman's attention. She waved the envelope in the air.

Cora watched her teacher take a deep breath and nod to Miss Kelly.

"Well then," Mrs. Bergman said, "Let's all go downstairs and hear what Mr. Bigg has to say."

Jimmie whispered to Cora on the way down, "This is it."

George took Ruby's hand, and Laszlo smiled at Tito and walked beside him. Tito didn't act friendly, but he didn't tell Laszlo to leave him alone.

When all the students were settled, Miss Kelly slit the white envelope with a letter opener, which she had brought with her. She shook the paper open and her eyes scanned the typed words. She frowned and cleared her throat.

"Here's his answer," she said and began to read.

Dear Children of Cherry Pit Junction:

Thank you for your recent letters. I am pleased that you understand how business is conducted, and have brought these issues to my attention.

However, at the present time, I will not be making any changes in the status of the building you have mentioned.

In addition, let me point out that making repairs to the housing structure, without my permission, although seemingly a noble gesture, would legally constitute vandalism. All such activities will be reported to law enforcement.

Yours truly,

*Harold L. Bigg*

Harold L. Bigg

The room went quiet. Then a hum of whispers began and hands shot up all over the room.

"All right, all right," Miss Kelly said. "I'm sure many of you would like to say something, but since this concerns Tito the most, I think we'll let him begin. Please quiet down and listen. Tito?"

Tito stood. His face was expressionless. "I do not know why I let you make me think anything could be different for us." He sat down. Then he stood right back up. "But, but *Mamá* said we... I want to say... *gracias* for the beds and stove. Thank you." He sat down again and stayed in his seat.

Other hands were raised immediately. The teacher called on a girl named Louise.

"That's just mean that he won't let anyone fix his old building," she said.

"It does seem that way, but as owner he certainly has the right to say that," Mrs. Bergman explained.

Cora was called on next. "Mr. Bigg didn't even tell us the reason he won't do anything," she complained. "If we'd written something like that he'd call us rude."

"Yes, that's probably true," Miss Kelly said. "Adults often think they don't need to treat children with respect. George?"

George looked thoughtful. "I think maybe Mr. Bigg doesn't care about anything except money. He knows people will work in the factory, and they won't need a car if they live close by, so they put up with the broken things."

"That's possible," Miss Kelly said. "Anyone else?"

A sixth grader named Bill was called on. "It might not be such a good thing if the buildings were fixed. Maybe Mr. Bigg would pay people less in the factory if he has to spend a lot on repairs."

"That's an interesting idea. Does anyone have something to say about this? Yes, Javier?"

Javier's family had lived and worked in many places, and he knew some of the laws the factories had to follow. He said, "There is a law that says he can not pay less to most of the workers. It's called 'minimum wage,' which is seventy-five cents an hour. Some of the foremen get more, and I guess he could cut their pay, but he has to pay us the minimum even if he doesn't like our brown skin."

"Very good," Miss Kelly said. "Labor laws protect people from unscrupulous companies." She turned and wrote "unscrupulous: without moral principles, unfair or dishonest" on the blackboard. The children in grades four through six instantly knew they'd have to learn to spell that word before Friday.

Javier raised his hand again, and was recognized. "I still think this man does not like people who are dark. I'm sure he pays Mr. Dubois more than seventy-five cents." He looked at Cora with a sneer.

Ruby's hand shot up, and the teacher called on her. Her feisty attitude was clear in her steady voice. She faced Javier. "I don't think it has anything to do with a person's color. Our father got offered a job there all winter because he does good work, and understands the machines. And we are lots browner than you are."

While Ruby spoke, Miss Kelly added to the blackboard the word "discrimination: to treat people unequally based on their race or beliefs."

"It's time for lunch, children. You may be dismissed to get your lunchboxes. I'm sure none of you will discriminate against other students because of race," Mrs. Bergman said.

Javier and Cora glared at each other across the room, but it had nothing to do with skin color.

## 11. THE PADLOCKED HEART

Tito ate his lunch quickly, ran outside and then grabbed Javier by the sleeve. He pulled him to the edge of the playground and whispered to him in Spanish. The two boys ducked behind some bushes at the edge of the school property.

"I need your help," Tito said. "I found something, but I can't read it all. It's in cursive."

He pulled Kitty's letter out of his lunch pail and handed it to Javier.

"Where did you get this?" the older boy asked.

Tito was wary, as he usually was, of anyone he might not be able to boss around. He avoided answering the question. "It's old. No one cares if we read it."

"How old?"

# The Dubois Files
# by Joan H. Young

Chapter mysteries for young readers, suggested grade level 3rd and up. Each book approximately 20,000 words.

The Dubois Files combine adventure and mystery without being violent or dark. They are set in the mid-twentieth century when moral standards were generally expected to be upheld, and the children will sometimes be presented with opportunities to choose between right and wrong in the context of the times.

The primary characters include Jimmie Mosher, of English descent; Cora Dubois with a Finnish mother and French father; Laszlo Szep, the son of a Hungarian tenant farmer; and George and Ruby Harris, a brother and sister of African-American ancestry. These ethnicities fit into the time and place without straining credulity. Of course, the extended families, and associated problems, will come into the plots.

From an elementary educator: "The "mysteries" are intriguing and not without danger. Bravo."

Anastasia Raven
Mysteries
by
Joan H. Young

at Amazon, Smashwords, Barnes & Noble, Kobo,
iBooks and selected bookstores
paperback or ebook

booksleavingfootprints.com

"I can read the date. It's 1930. Twenty-three years ago; I subtracted. It's the middle part that's too hard."

Javier removed the pink letter from the pink envelope and smelled it. "Pink is from girls. No perfume, though."

"I told you it's old," Tito said, feeling annoyed. "And I already know it was written by a girl, or maybe a woman, named Kitty."

Javier read out loud:

Dearest Harry,

I'm writing to you again although I still can't mail the letters to you. I'm putting them in my secret Post Office until I see you. My father locks the door on the inside with a padlock at night, and he watches me every minute during the day. I feel like he has padlocked my heart. I wish he would take us to California where so many of our friends have gone. It's warm there all the time. Maybe I could run away to you while we are on the road.

Mother cries every day. We are so poor now.

Just then, Miss Kelly rang the bell that signaled the end of lunch break. Javier tried to put the letter in his pocket, but Tito grabbed it away.

"There's more," Javier said and snorted. "A girl with a padlocked heart! I'll bet the rest is full of kisses and mushy stuff."

"You can read it later," Tito answered stubbornly. "It's mine."

"Put it to good use. Someone might pay you money to get this," Javier said with a wicked grin. "Maybe this Kitty is no longer poor, and she wouldn't want her friends to know she lived in that smelly building and did hard work for almost no pay."

Tito did not know the word "blackmail," but somehow he understood that asking a person for money to get a letter that belonged to them anyway was wrong.

He liked Javier. Well, he didn't exactly like the older boy, but he wanted to have the kind of power Javier seemed to hold over the rest of the Mexican boys and girls. He certainly didn't want Javier to think he was a chicken or weak.

"I will look for Harry and Kitty," he answered.

And that was exactly what he planned to do. But the more he thought about what he should do if he found one or both of them, the more he decided that Javier had the kind of heart his mother had told him was bad. It was a problem. Tito wanted, very much wanted, to be the man in charge. But he thought that if he didn't pray for a clean heart, he might end up being a lot like Mr. Bigg.

He headed back toward the classroom. In one of the trash cans he saw notebook paper like the older children used. Although the bell had already rung, Tito stopped and picked through the discarded pages, looking for some that had a blank back side. When he had several, he ran to the classroom and slid into his seat.

"Tito, you are late," Mrs. Bergman chided.

"Sorry, Teacher," he said. He almost told her he'd been in the bathroom, but his recent thoughts about dark and light hearts kept him from telling the lie.

Throughout the afternoon, whenever there was a free minute between lessons, Tito copied the cursive letters that were displayed on the wall. He didn't dare use up the precious clean paper Ruby had given him, so he worked carefully to make the writing fit on the backs of the used sheets he had found.

"I will read Kitty's letters without any help from Javier," he said to himself.

## 12. DEVELOPING A PLAN

"Your house, four o'clock," Jimmie said to Cora as he and Laszlo got off the school bus.

"We'll be there too," George said.

The boys changed clothes and did their afternoon chores together, helping each other as they checked the late tomatoes in the garden for big green worms. They made sure there was clean straw mulch under the ripening red globes to help stop them from splitting. At Laszlo's house, they brought in fresh drinking water and swept the dried mud out of the back porch where Mr. Szep took off his field boots and jackets.

At quarter to four they jumped on their bikes and pedaled to Cora's house. She, along with George and Ruby, were waiting on the back porch.

"We made lemonade," Cora called.

Even though it was late September, the afternoon was warm. The drinks felt sparkly and cool on their throats, which were dry from the dusty bicycle ride.

They sat side by side on the high edge of the concrete slab, banging their heels against the wall.

Ruby sneezed. "Hay fever, I'll bet"

"You don't even know what that is, Ruby." George changed the subject to the one they were all thinking of. "What are we going to do about Mr. Bigg?"

"He sure sounds unfriendly," Laszlo said.

Cora was always looking for solutions. "Maybe he doesn't really know how bad things are. My dad said he hasn't been here in years."

"How can we get him to come?" Ruby asked.

Jimmie jumped off the edge of the porch and whirled around. "We can take the building to him!"

"What on earth do you mean?" Cora asked.

"Pictures," Jimmie said. "Your folks have a camera, right? We'll take photos of all the things wrong with the building. Then we'll send them to Mr. Bigg."

Cora stood up. "I have a better idea. Here comes Papa. I hear the car. Let me ask him something."

Philippe Dubois was indeed pulling in beside the house.

Cora ran to greet him. He leaned down and kissed his daughter and gave her his briefcase so he could remove his suit jacket. She took his hand and pulled him toward her friends. "We want to ask you something," she said.

"What's up?" Mr. Dubois asked, carefully folding the coat across his arm.

The other children pointed at Cora. "It's her party," George said.

The kitchen door squealed and Reeta Dubois came outside. "You children shouldn't be pestering a man the minute he gets home from work. He's tired. Give him a few minutes."

"Mom! It's important," Cora insisted.

"Well, come inside and talk then, so he can at least put his feet up," she replied, holding the door open.

Mr. Dubois winked at Cora. "I am tired, but you're my favorite kiddo," he joked.

"I'm your only kiddo," Cora said, but she laughed happily at the familiar line.

On his way through the kitchen, Cora's father hung his jacket on the back of a kitchen chair, loosened his necktie and unfastened the top button of his shirt. In the living room, he let himself down into an easy chair and leaned forward.

"Almost ready," he said, untying his shoes.

The children stood in a semi-circle around the large ottoman that matched the chair. As soon as Mr. Dubois had his shoes off and his feet up, they explained.

"Mr. Bigg said he wouldn't do anything at all about that building," Jimmie began.

In just a few minutes they had told him about the letter and their idea to take pictures.

Cora's mother brought her husband a cup of coffee. She said, "I've been listening, too, and I think it's a good idea. We do have a camera, but we'll have to get some film in town tomorrow. Philippe?"

"But my idea is even better than what you've heard," Cora said. "I didn't finish."

"Tell us," George said.

"I think we should take the pictures to Mr. Bigg in person. He didn't even explain why he won't do anything. If he has to face us, we'll be harder to ignore. Right, Papa?"

"That's probably true," Mr. Dubois admitted.

"Could you take us to the city? Please, Papa."

Ruby did a little dance. George wanted to know how long it took to drive to Cold Rapids. Laszlo told him it was two hours each way. His family had gone there to catch the train to Chicago in August.

But Jimmie was the realist. He frowned. "There's no way we can do it unless we skip school. Mr. Bigg won't be in his office on the weekend."

"That's true, but maybe this really is important," Cora's father said.

"If we take pictures tomorrow after school, how fast will the film be developed?" Jimmie asked.

Mrs. Dubois answered. "The drugstore has one day service. If I drop the film off Wednesday morning, I can pick up the pictures on Thursday."

"I don't know if we can get an appointment to see Mr. Bigg on Friday, but I'll try," Mr. Dubois said.

"Hooray!" George yelled. "We'll ask our teachers if we can miss one school day."

It was after five-thirty. Cora was already home, but the others raced for their bicycles so they wouldn't be late for supper.

\*\*\*

That night, as Cora was brushing her teeth she overheard her mother say to her father, "Cora and her friends have big hearts, but

Harold Bigg is a hard man. I hope you don't lose your job."

## 13. TITO'S LESSONS

Tito sat at the table in his kitchen. It was the short broken one with potato crates for chairs, but he was small and the size was comfortable. Also, there was an electric light in the kitchen. His math workbook was open in front of him. He'd almost finished the page he was supposed to do for homework, but he couldn't wait any longer. The pink envelope was calling to him.

He removed the letter and spread it out. Placing a sheet of white paper over it, he could just make out the words on the pink page. He traced over them, transferring the letters to the white paper. He thought if he could feel the shapes as he made them, it would be easier to read. It was a good idea. Tito quickly began to understand how the cursive letters were similar to the printed ones. There weren't too many that were really different. He smiled. This was going to be easier than he thought.

He hadn't bothered to copy the part Javier had read. He saw the words clearly now. The second half of Kitty's letter said:

*The work is very hard. Today we picked asparagus. Hours and hours lying on our stomachs on a thing like an airplane wing pulled by a tractor. We never used to do work like this. Now I'll appreciate asparagus more when I eat it!*

*My neck is stiff. I wish you could rub it for me and make it all better. Kisses would be so nice too. Oh, Harry! I miss you ever so much.*

After that were a line of Xs and Os, followed by the closing he had read before:

*I love you, Kitty Perham.*

Tito thought about this letter. Apparently Kitty's family hadn't always been poor. He wondered what could have happened to make them have to live in this place and work in the fields. And he knew just how she felt about the asparagus, although he didn't like the taste very much.

There was no clock in his house, but Tito glanced out the back window. The sunlight was almost gone. Soon his mother would cook supper, plain tortillas with some refried beans and cheese. He hoped there would be a cup of hot cocoa with cinnamon for dessert, but maybe the sugar was all gone. They only had powdered milk from the government, but the cinnamon helped cover the funny taste. He sighed and finished his math problems, then went in the other room to watch the babies while his mother cooked.

Later, when Marco was settled in the playpen and Francesca was curled under a blanket in the new bed, Tito sat in the kitchen, sipping the hoped-for cup of hot chocolate. His mother was washing the baby's diapers.

"*Mamá*, what could have happened in 1930 to make someone suddenly so poor they might have to live like we do and work in the fields and factory?"

"That is a serious question for such a small boy, *miijo*,"[9] Rosa Gonzales said. "Why do you ask this?"

"I read something," Tito said.

"That was a long time ago. I would have been two years old. Can you picture *Mamá* as a baby?"

Tito laughed. "That is funny! Did you look like Francesca?"

---

[9] say MEE-hoe. My son in Spanish

"I think I looked more like Marco, but we have no pictures to help us remember."

"But, how could a man lose all his money back then?" Tito asked again.

"There were some very bad times in the United States. My *papá* told me. Something happened with the banks in 1929, and many people no longer had enough money to live. White people worked beside the dark ones in the fields. Children died. Many of them drove all the way to California because even the land dried up and blew away. The Americans have words for those years. The Great Depression and the Dust Bowl, they call them."

"That must have been a very bad time," Tito said.

"*Si, muy mal*,"[10] she answered, putting a hand on Tito's arm. "Is your homework done?"

"Almost, *Mamá*."

"Turn out the light when you have finished." Rosa entered the main room and climbed into the second twin bed the church people had

---

[10] Say MOO-ee MAHL. very bad in Spanish

brought. She thought about Tito's question, and even though her life was hard, she said a prayer of thanks for good soil and for people who were trying to help her remain where Tito could stay in school. She kissed her fingers and touched the crucifix that hung on the wall.

In the kitchen, Tito thought about the other letters. He got a knife and slit a second one open.

This one was dated April 1, 1930. *Earlier than the other one*, Tito thought. He had already become comfortable reading the cursive script. Kitty's writing was almost exactly like the examples he had copied from the schoolroom wall.

Dear Harry,

The movers took the last of our furniture away yesterday, and the bank owns the big house. The cash we had is all used up. Father says I must never see you again, that you are too good for us now. He is so proud! Too much so, I think. He won't let even let Mother's brother help us. Uncle Clarence said we could live with them, but Father wouldn't have it. He is so angry, and that makes him mean.

I wanted to mail this to you, but Father grabbed the letter away and tore it up, so I had to re-write it. Will I ever see you again?

"Tito! Come to bed," his mother called.

"*Si, Mamá*." Tito put the letters back in his workbook, stepped on a crate and pulled the string to turn out the light.

Francesca snuggled close to him when he climbed into the bed. His arm encircled the little girl and he prayed he wouldn't grow up to be like Kitty's father, or end up in jail, like his own *Papá*.

# 14. PHOTOGRAPHIC EVIDENCE

The rest of the week went by so fast Cora could hardly believe it.

Tuesday morning, the five friends explained to their teachers what they wanted to do, and asked if they could have Friday off. Of course everything depended on whether Mr. Bigg would actually agree to see them.

The teachers said they would need notes from their parents, and it would have to count as a family day. Students were allowed two of those each year. And they would still need to take the spelling test early and do their homework.

Everyone promised!

Cora's mother brought the camera to school with a new spool of film from the drugstore already loaded. She also had a box of flashbulbs. The camera was easy to use. You just looked through the little window at the back, held it really still, pressed a button and then turned a wheel to make the film roll forward inside the camera. If you forgot to do that after each picture, you'd get two pictures on top of each other, a double exposure.

The only thing that was tricky was using the flash for indoor pictures. There was a round silvery bowl that had to be mounted on the side of the camera. Then a flashbulb was pushed into a socket in the middle of the bowl. When you pushed the shutter button the bulb was supposed to flare and make a bright light so the picture wouldn't be too dark.

But sometimes the bulb failed to light up, ruining a picture. And it made a crunchy, crinkly kind of noise that was startling. You had to be careful to hold the camera still. And then the bulb was really hot! You could burn your fingers if you tried to change it too soon.

There were twelve possible exposures on the roll. Cora took two pictures of Tito sitting at his desk holding a pencil, with an open workbook. Then she took a picture of his whole class, with Mrs. Bergman.

When school let out for the day, the friends did not get on the school bus. They explained to the driver that they were going to visit the Gonzales family. Then they walked home with Tito. He had never had his picture taken before, and it made him feel important. It was also exciting to have so many older kids pay attention to him.

"We have nine pictures left," Cora said. "What should we use them for?"

"Two for the broken windows," Jimmie said.

"The light that's hanging loose," Ruby said.

Cora was counting on her fingers. "We're down to six."

"The whole kitchen, so he can see the open shelves and that there's no refrigerator," George suggested.

They were just reaching the long building. Laszlo looked up. "I think we need to show the entire row of houses. The paint is all blotchy and flaky."

"Four more," Cora said.

They had come to one of the doors. Tito asked them to wait, and in a minute he came out carrying the baby. Francesca tagged behind, sucking her thumb.

"Oh! Take that picture," Ruby said. "How could Mr. Bigg not like those cute babies?"

So Cora had Tito stand in front of his own door, holding Marco. Francesca reached up with her free hand and held on to Tito's shirt. The door with its cracked panels and the paint curling from the wall completed the background. She took two pictures, to be sure everyone was holding still in one of them.

Then she handed the camera to Jimmie. "You take the rest. This is a group project."

Jimmie went through the list they had made, pushing the shutter button, and carefully remembering to advance the film after every shot. They used the flash for all the inside pictures. Once, the flash didn't go off so they had to retake that picture.

George wondered why the church people had not brought a lamp the Gonzales family could use in the main room. But then he looked around. There were no electric outlets in the wall. "Hey, how do you plug things in?" he asked Tito.

"We don't," Tito answered simply. He was busy mixing up some powdered milk to fill the baby's bottle.

"There's one more picture left," Cora said. We have to finish the roll of film.

"Maybe when Tito's mom gets off work she should be in a picture. What time is it?" Laszlo asked.

No one knew.

They all walked to the factory to see Mr. Dubois and find out what time it was. The three oldest children took turns carrying Marco.

But there was still a lot of time before closing. Mr. Dubois suggested the Gonzales family stand together by the line of apples that was moving along the conveyors. Rosa picked up Francesca, and Tito took Marco again. Rosa's white apron and kerchief contrasted with the dark walls. All the machinery in the background of the picture emphasized how hard she worked.

"That's it," Cora said. Now we have to rewind the film and take it out of the camera.

"Thanks for helping us take the pictures, Tito," Ruby said.

"It's OK. Maybe it's not your fault we are in trouble," he answered.

Tito turned and began to walk toward his house, Francesca still clinging to his shirt.

## 15. KITTY UNDERSTANDS

When Tito reached his house he looked at it differently. It was as if he could see the photographs they had just taken, colorless snapshots of damage and pain. He thought of the lady named Kitty. She had felt it too.

He turned Francesca loose to run with the other children who roamed freely around the building. He looked at the inside of the door casing and found the screw holes where Kitty's father must have had the hasp and lock to keep her shut up. He rubbed a finger across the rough edges of the holes.

Then he changed Marco's diaper and put the dirty one in a bucket of water to soak. *My whole life is a dirty stinking diaper*, he thought.

He spread a blanket on the dirt in front of his door and lowered Marco onto it. The baby sat up, looked at Tito with big brown eyes and stuck his thumb in his mouth.

Maybe Kitty could help him understand. She hadn't always lived here. He went inside and slit open another of the pink envelopes, grabbing the gingerbread-man doll on the way back out. Marco held out his arms and hugged the doll when his big brother handed it to him.

Tito sat in the dirt, leaning against the cool concrete wall so he could keep an eye on the younger children, and unfolded the letter.

October 4, 1930

Harry my Darling,

Father stepped over the line today. He slapped mother—all she did was ask if we could go to church. When I tried to protect her, he grabbed me by the wrist

and twisted it so badly I thought
it might be broken. I guess not,
but now it's purple and swollen.
He doesn't understand I'm no
longer a child.

We need you to come help us!
Don't you care about me any more?

Tito thought: *In a few days, it will be exactly twenty-three years ago that this happened. And her father did bad things, too. But he probably did not go to jail. Nobody goes to jail for slapping a woman. But I do not think anyone should slap Cora or Ruby. They would hit back. And I would not like it if someone hurt* Mamá *or* Francesca. *Maybe a good man would find another way to tell his family he was not happy.*

He slowly read the rest of the letter:

It's so hard, not hearing from you for months. I like to dream that you are writing to me. Maybe Father is taking your letters before I see them. It's as if he's gone crazy—so worried about his precious reputation he can't let us enjoy even little pleasures, like seeing old friends.

I don't know where we are going when the apples are done. I'm so sick of apples! I hope I never have to smell one again. But we'll be leaving here. I'm always *scheming to run away and come to you.*

*As ever,*

*X X X O O O*

*Kitty*

Tito worked hard to sound out rep-u-ta-tion. He didn't know what that meant, but Kitty's father seemed to love it more than his family. He couldn't figure out scheming at all, but in every letter Kitty was trying to find a way to escape the padlocked door and get to Harry.

Francesca ran up and grabbed him around the knees with dirty hands. "Tito! *Agua!*" she demanded. The others gathered around also begging for drinks. He stuffed Kitty's letter in a pocket and led them to the kitchen. There he washed little hands and faces and filled glass after glass with rusty water from the tap until they were satisfied.

Left outside, Marco began to cry. Tito mixed some dry milk with water and filled a baby bottle.

*Maybe he wasn't like Kitty.* Papá *didn't hurt them and hold them behind a lock. Or did he? Stealing things and going to jail had hurt* Mamá. *She had to work all the time now. Watching Francesca and Marco meant he couldn't play in the afternoons. Maybe that was a little bit like being locked up. He didn't want to run away. But he did want to run away from this kind of life. He was glad they were staying where he could go to school for the whole year.*

Papá *could barely read English. But he could. And hadn't he just taught himself to read cursive? Maybe he was a smart boy. Maybe he could be a good man and not be angry with people.*

Tito sighed and took the bottle to Marco. That was all the deep thinking he could do for one day. He grabbed his reading book and began the assigned story while there was still daylight.

## 16. BIGG BUCKS

Reeta Dubois picked up the developed photographs at the drugstore Thursday afternoon, and then stopped at the school to tell Cora she should go to her father's office after classes. Jimmie and George were in the same classroom, so Cora managed to signal them about the plan.

The three older children waited for Laszlo and Ruby when school let out, so they wouldn't get on the bus. Then they crossed the road and walked to the canning factory.

Once in the office, Mr. Dubois handed a thick envelope to Cora.

"This was your idea, Jimmie. You open it," she said.

Jimmie took out his pocket knife and slit the seal. Inside was a booklet of their pictures and the plastic strips with the negatives that could be used to make more copies. He carefully tore the photos out of the book along the perforations so they could spread them on the desk. All but one was crisp and had good contrast. The fuzzy one didn't matter because it was of Tito with his workbook, and they had taken two of those.

Ruby picked up one of the plastic strips and held it up toward a window. "Hey, these are weird. Everything that should be dark is light."

"That's why it's called a negative," Cora said. "All the tones are the opposite of the picture."

"Look at this one," George said, putting his finger on a photo.

It was the picture of the Gonzales children in front of their door. A corner of the window with its dark crack was visible as were the broken door panels and peeling paint. The children looked lost and sad. The angle of the afternoon light had made the shadows dramatic. Mr. Dubois thought it was a striking photograph, maybe good enough to be published in a magazine. The one of Rosa Gonzales in the factory was equally good.

"I have some news for you," Cora's father said. "Mr. Bigg has agreed to meet with you at one in the afternoon tomorrow. I'll treat you to lunch in Cold Rapids, and then take you to his office. It's in the Bigg Building."

"Wow!" Jimmie and Laszlo said together.

"Hooray!" George yelled.

Cora and Ruby grabbed hands and whirled around until Cora's braids stuck out straight behind her.

"Wear your best school clothes. I'm sure Mr. Bigg will have on a suit and tie."

"We will," they all chorused.

"Here's something else I found that might interest you." Mr. Dubois reached into a drawer and brought out a manila folder.

Jimmie put the photos and negatives back in their envelope to make room for the contents of the file. Laszlo opened it and discovered that it was filled with newspaper clippings. Some were quite new, but others were brown and brittle with a sharp smell that made his nose itch. They appeared to all be about Mr. Bigg, and many had a heading: "Society Column."

They laid the cuttings on the desk and looked them over, reading anything that caught their attention.

Ruby loved nice clothes and was immediately drawn to a picture of a young man in a dark suit beside a shapely woman. She had her gloved hand on the man's arm. Even in the yellowed newspaper photo it was obvious the dress was sparkly, and the woman wore a lot of shiny jewelry. Ruby traced the caption with her finger and read, "Harold L. Bigg and his wife, Kathryn

Perham Bigg, entering the ballroom for the grand opening of the Bigg Building."

There were more pictures, including recent ones. Mr. Bigg had gained weight. He had one son, a college boy, who looked a lot like the older picture of his father.

Cora was trying to read some of the articles that didn't have pictures. Phrases like "capital investments," and "corporate amalgamation" didn't mean much to her. But then she whistled. "Listen to this, 'Bigg's net worth is estimated to be one-million, two-hundred thousand dollars.'"

In the car, as Mr. Dubois took them home, George thought Mr. Bigg was very rich and very fat. But George felt very poor and very small. He wondered if the others felt the same.

## 17. THE BIGG BUILDING

The children huddled around Mr. Dubois as they stepped into the Bigg Building elevator. "Fifth floor," he said.

"Step to the back of the car," ordered a tiny old man in a red jacket.

Only Cora had been there before. The scents of old, stained carpet and greased cables combined to produce an odor she never forgot. Cora rubbed her nose and adjusted the white blouse beneath her jumper where it had ridden up into her armpits.

The man reached forward and pushed down on a jointed bar that closed and locked the outer door. Then he stepped back and slid a brass gate across the front of the car. The gate showed a diamond pattern when it was closed. There was a brass shape like an upside down soup bowl fastened to the wall. It had a handle sticking out of the top. The man slid the handle to the left along the edge of the circle.

They heard a thump and a distant motor began to whine, rising in pitch. The floor jerked.

As oldest, Jimmie wanted to act sophisticated, and he tried hard not to reach out and grab the brass rail that encircled the small square room. *This paneling is real wood. Maybe walnut*, he thought. *I wonder if Mr. Bigg will listen to us. We're just farm kids.*

George and Ruby had never even been to Cold Rapids. Ruby stood with her mouth open, gazing at the ceiling. She whispered, "George, how can that light work when we're moving?"

"Electricity. See there are lights over there too." her brother pointed beyond the old operator to a panel with glowing buttons marked with words like "stop," and "call". "I don't know how they fasten the wires to a room that moves."

"The wires connect to the top of the car. They have to be as long as the elevator shaft is tall," Cora's father explained.

Laszlo had been in elevators in New York City, when his family had first come from Hungary. Memories of those visits to stuffy offices, and the slowing and bumpy adjustment when the elevator came to a stop made his stomach lurch. He hoped Mr. Bigg wouldn't be as unfriendly as some of the men his family had met with.

The diamonds of brass mesh scissored and disappeared when the operator opened the gate. As he released the outer door and slid it back, he announced, "Five."

They stepped soundlessly into an empty hallway covered in dark green carpet. Ruby tugged on Mr. Dubois' coat sleeve. "I have to pee," she said.

"Let's all be sure we are calm and prepared," said Mr. Dubois, as he led them toward the rest rooms.

\*\*\*

The frosted glass on the door had "Harold L. Bigg, walk in" painted in gold letters. Mr. Dubois turned the knob and they entered a large bright space with green carpet and orange curtains. There were padded chairs around the edge of the room. The secretary, a woman wearing a blue suit, was seated at a desk. Arranged around her were two telephones, a typewriter, a brown box with dials and little levers, jars of pencils and pens, and a vase of orange and yellow chrysanthemums.

"May I help you?" she asked, smiling.

Mr. Dubois nodded at Jimmie.

"We have an appointment to see Mr. Bigg," Jimmie said. He wanted to sound confident, but his voice squeaked a little.

George went to a window and looked out. He could see straight down the side of the red brick building, and over the city, stretching to the horizon. Cold Rapids was a big place, and George was already uncomfortable. A pigeon on the ledge stared at him with a beady black eye.

## 18. MR. BIGG

"He's expecting you. Come right along," the secretary said. She asked their names and then rose from her seat and opened another door in the back wall.

The children filed in. A giant of a man stood and waited while the woman introduced each of them. Then he spoke in a deep voice, "Hello, children. Philippe." He shook hands with Mr. Dubois and sat down. Mr. Dubois moved to back to the doorway. He planned to let the children do the talking.

Someone had arranged several small wooden chairs, the kind from the school library, in front of Mr. Bigg's desk. Jimmie, George, and Ruby sat. Cora and Laszlo remained standing. Smoke from the cigar, which was nestled between two of Mr. Bigg's huge fingers, curled upward. Laszlo coughed.

Cora took a deep breath and concentrated to remember words her father had suggested she use. She removed the photographs from their envelope and placed them in a line on the desk, turned so they were right side up for Mr. Bigg to see. "We'd like to talk to you about the housing for people who work at the Cherry Pit Junction canning factory," she began. "We brought pictures, in case you haven't seen the condition of the building lately."

"We took photographs of the things that need repairs right away," Jimmie said. "Our letters explained them, but these snapshots really show the problems."

George stood up and arranged the pictures so the ones with Tito were together. "Here's Tito at school, and these are of his family. They want to stay here so he can finish the school year. They work hard, but their house isn't warm or clean. And I think the electricity isn't safe." He sat down.

Mr. Bigg pushed the pictures around with a fat finger. He tapped his cigar on the edge of an ashtray. He cleared his throat. "Let me remind you that this housing is provided free of charge to workers."

"But..." Ruby said.

Mr. Bigg held up a hand to silence her. "If the people who lived there took care of the structures, instead of treating them with disrespect, the conditions would be satisfactory. I can't be expected to repeatedly fix things which temporary residents wantonly destroy."

Ruby was not so easily put off. "What about heat?" she said.

"I certainly have no intention of winterizing the building. The work season does not extend to the colder months, and it would be a waste of money to provide heat."

"Could our fathers install a wood stove? They know how," Laszlo asked, remembering that the teacher had said to offer suggestions.

The brown box beside Mr. Bigg buzzed. He reached over and pushed down a lever. "Yes?"

The secretary's voice came through a speaker. "Dana is here to see you now."

"Give me two minutes." He turned back to Laszlo. "Definitely not. That would encourage unsavory riff-raff to live there in the winter."

Cora couldn't believe they had traveled all this way, and would only be allowed two more minutes. She began to explain what a hard worker Mrs. Gonzales was.

George suggested there might be some job Tito's mother could do through the winter months.

The young man they knew from reading the newspapers to be Mr.Bigg's son entered through the open door. They gathered the photos, and the secretary hustled them out of the room. Mr. Bigg did not even say, "Good day."

Everyone was silent as the elevator descended to the ground floor. Cora moved close to her father and turned her head. She didn't want Jimmie to see that tears were streaming down her cheeks.

## 19. DANA'S BIRTHDAY

Dana Bigg studied the crestfallen faces of the children as they left. He knew they weren't the first visitors to feel this way after talking with his father.

"Sit down," Mr. Bigg said. "Happy birthday."

"Thanks, Dad. I suppose that means I have to sign those papers today."

"Of course. You're twenty-one now. Half of this business is yours."

Dana squirmed. "I don't see much point in it. I'm not interested in being a business tycoon."

"You're my only child. I've worked my whole life for this, and you'll sign. You like the flashy sports car, and the nice clothes, and vacations in the Caribbean. Do you want to lose those?"

Dana sighed and accepted the pen his father handed him. He did like having money. He'd never lived any other way. When he finished, he said, "I couldn't help overhearing what those kids were asking about. Why don't you just clean up that old building before you get in trouble with housing codes or something?"

His father stabbed at the air with his cigar. "I'm not going to listen to some small-town brats who want me to help a hoodlum's family. There are no codes that far out in the country."

"What if you get reported? That man who brought the kids looked respectable."

"That's the girl's father. Dubois is a decent manager and I'll give him the benefit of the doubt and assume he's humoring that feisty daughter of his. But if he starts to get pushy, I'll replace him. Managers are a dime a dozen."

Dana thought briefly about arguing with his father. It was kind of fun to make the man angry and watch him fume. But Dana had problems of his own to think about.

He left the office, nodded to the secretary and headed for the apartment he was trying to rent for his senior year in college.

The young man hopped into his bright yellow 1953 Nash-Healy sports car and sped off in the direction of his hoped-for apartment. College classes had begun several weeks ago, but Dana had put off finding a place near campus to live.

Now all the good apartments or rooms were taken. He had found an available basement apartment only two blocks from where most of his classes were, but it was in terrible condition.

The windows leaked and the walls were stained and damp. The moisture had made the doors warp, and the whole place smelled musty. That was the reason no one had rented it yet. He'd been discussing the situation with the landlord, but the man refused to fix anything because he said college kids just made a mess anyway.

This man was being as stubborn as his father about fixing a building where people needed to live. Maybe his dad was planning to sell the Cherry Pit Junction property in the next year. But that didn't make much sense. The canning factory made a good profit, and he knew there

were plans to reconstruct the loading entrance
and make other repairs over the winter.

Dana was feeling annoyed. He wanted to find
a solution to his housing problem. But, since he
had always been rich, he thought of ways money
could be used to fix things. He said to himself: I
don't have to argue with this man. I'll get my
dad to buy the building. Hey! I just signed
papers saying I own half of Bigg, Inc. I can buy
the building myself.

His thoughts wandered away as he tried to
count how many buildings he and his father
now owned. Of course, there was the Bigg
Building, but he knew there were other canning
factories. He'd visited some of them on business
trips. He'd actually been in some of the other
housing units. Although none of them were
fancy, all the others were decent places to live,
which was curious. Why wouldn't his father fix
the building at Cherry Pit Junction?

## 20. DANA'S FIRST IDEA

It was an unusually hot Sunday afternoon for the first weekend of October, and Cora was lying across her bed propped on her elbows. The window was open and the breeze billowed the white curtains. She was making a list of the things that would need to be purchased to fix up the migrant building. She thought if she could add up what it would cost, maybe it wouldn't be very much, and she could ask Mr. Bigg again why he wouldn't spend even that amount of money.

She had written paint--how many cans? And glass—two panes? Refrigerator, furnace, and had just put down electrical parts--ask George or his father, when there was a knock on the front door. Cora jumped. If a car had turned off the road it must have been very quiet. She heard her mother answer the door and say "May

I help you?" in a voice that was reserved for people she did not know. Cora ran to the bottom of the stairs and waited. The young man she had seen in Mr. Bigg's office, his son, was standing on her front porch.

Cora heard him say "Is this the Dubois household? My name is Dana Bigg. I'm looking for Mr. Philippe Dubois, and I believe he has a daughter."

Cora thought her mother looked confused, but she politely invited the man in and called "Philippe? Cora?"

The tall boy, he didn't really look grown-up, stepped forward to shake Mr. Dubois' hand.

Cora came to her father's side. "My name is Cora," she said, holding out her own hand. Dana grinned and shook hands with Cora treating her with equal respect, although shaking hands with little girls was not a common practice for grown-up men, or even almost grown-up men.

"I'm sorry to barge in on your Sunday afternoon," Dana began, "but I couldn't help hear some of what you told my father. I think maybe I can help."

The almost immediate result was that Cora got to ride beside Dana in his cute yellow sports car. They first drove to George and Ruby's house and then to Jimmy and Lazlo's, and then all five friends rode in the convertible, with the top down, as Dana drove around a big country block. The warm air ruffled their hair. This was like riding in the back of the pickup truck, only much more fun.

Finally they returned to Cora's house. The children's faces were flushed with pleasure and the heat.

Cora's mother said, "May I offer you some coffee, Mr. Bigg?"

Dana looked around. "Oh, you mean me. I don't think I can get used to being called that name. Please use 'Dana.' And, I've never developed a taste for coffee."

"Some lemonade, then? It's a warm day, and I'm sure the children would like it."

"That sounds swell," Dana said with a smile.

In a few minutes the children were sitting cross-legged on Cora's living room floor, holding cold glasses of pale yellow Kool-Aid. Philippe and Reeta Dubois shared the couch and Dana sat in the matching chair.

"My dad can be really difficult sometimes," Dana said. "But I don't understand why he's being so stubborn this time. I've been to some of the other factories, and this housing is much more run down. It's as if my father dislikes this one in particular, and won't fix it up."

"How can we change his mind?" George asked.

Dana looked thoughtful. He glanced at Philippe. "I don't think anything ordinary will move him to action. I have an idea, but, Mr. Dubois, you'll need to approve of it. I'm pretty sure it will make my father angry. He might take it out on you."

"Let's at least hear it," Philippe said.

"All right. May I see the photographs you had? I only caught a glimpse of them in the office."

Cora ran upstairs and returned in a minute with the envelope. She pulled out the pictures and separated them into two piles. "These are the ones of broken stuff," she said, handing them to Dana.

He shuffled through them and nodded. "But you have others, I think. These wouldn't have given my father the worried look I saw on his face."

"Yes we do," Jimmie said. "And we think they show how hard Tito's family works. They are sad pictures."

Dana took the ones of Rosa at the factory, Tito with Francesca and Marco, and Tito at school. He looked at the children with sparkling eyes. "You took these? They're dynamite!"

"I took this one," Jimmie said pointing to the one in the factory. "Cora took the others."

"A photographer's eye. Good job, you two. I can get these published easily. People like my dad, who think they are really important, hate negative publicity. He'll be falling over himself;

he'll be in such a rush to fix that building after these appear in print."

Reeta Dubois shifted in her chair and frowned. "I don't like this idea very much," she said. "My husband might be fired if Mr. Bigg, Harold Bigg, feels threatened by our family. That won't help anybody."

"Gosh, George and Ruby's dad could lose his job too, if Mr. Bigg gets mad at us," Laszlo said. "He knows we took those pictures."

"I can see your point," Dana admitted.

Everyone sat in uncomfortable silence.

Ruby got up and put her hands on the arm of the overstuffed chair. She looked Dana in the eyes. "Please, Mr. Dana, we want to help Tito. I was mad at him at first, but it's so sad how he lives."

Dana snapped his fingers. "Jeepers Creepers! I keep forgetting. There is another way.

## 21. DANA'S SECOND IDEA

"I forgot to tell you it was my birthday the same day you came to see my dad. I'm twenty-one now."

"Happy birthday," Reeta Dubois said politely.

"Happy birthday," everyone chorused.

Ruby was puzzled. "Does your birthday have something to do with Tito's problem?"

"You'll see," Dana said. "But I also have to tell you about my apartment."

"Why?" Laszlo asked.

"Be patient, and it will make sense. I've been complaining to the man who owns the building where I want to live this semester. It's got leaking windows and the walls are moldy."

"Ick. Then why do you want to live there?" Ruby asked.

"Why do people want to live in Cherry Pit Junction?" Dana responded with a question of his own.

"Because it's where the factory is," George said. "We talked about that in school."

Dana grinned. "Exactly. So this man who owns the house thinks students just bust things up anyway, so he won't clean it up. But he knows it will eventually rent because the house is close to campus."

"What's your point?" Jimmie asked.

"I think this landlord sounds like your dad," Cora said. "But how does this help us?"

"It helps because I was so mad at this guy I was ready to buy the building and fix it up myself. And maybe I will do just that."

Philippe Dubois chuckled and nodded. Everyone else still looked confused.

Dana pointed a finger at Cora's father. "You got it. Dad forced me to sign papers making me a partner in Bigg, Inc. on my birthday. I am officially an adult and now half-owner of all the properties, including the one at Cherry Pit

Junction. If I want to make some repairs, he can't stop me."

"You would do that?" George asked, jumping to his feet.

"I would!" Dana said, slapping his hand on the arm of the chair. "Maybe he'll be angry enough to drop me as a partner afterwards. That would be just fine with me. I'm not a suit-and-tie kind of guy."

*\*\**

The following weekend was three days long because there was no school on Monday, Columbus Day.

Early Saturday morning a pickup truck came to a stop in front of the green building at Cherry Pit Junction. The back was filled with ladders, cans of paint, brushes, and tools of all kinds. Two young men spilled out the truck doors. Dana, in his yellow sports car, pulled in behind them. Riding with him were the five friends, although the top of the convertible was up today. The sky was clear and deep blue, but the heat of the previous week had broken, and autumn orange and gold glowed in the trees.

More trucks and cars began to arrive. Laszlo's father came in his pickup truck, the back filled with lumber and nails, and the Szep family riding in the front. The Harrises, Dubois, and Moshers were all there, too.

Francesca ran up to Laszlo's little sister Eniko and demanded, "Play with me." Eniko saw the pull-toy that used to be hers and soon the two little girls were giggling and running around the building dragging the wiggling dog.

Tito and the older children who lived in the building were more interested in the various trucks than toys.

"What's going to happen today?" they asked in mixtures of English and Spanish. Everyone had already heard that big changes were going to be made in the building.

One of Dana's friends, Ken, was studying to be an architect, but he spent the summers doing construction work to earn money for college. He took charge. Of course, a lot of planning had taken place since the previous Sunday when Dana decided to take action.

"You won't believe this is the same place in a couple of days!" Ken exclaimed, pulling a stepladder from the truck. "Here, you. You're tall. Step up there and start scraping." He handed Javier a wire brush and showed him how to clean the flaking paint off the concrete blocks.

Soon everyone was doing some sort of job, whether it was unloading a truck, scraping paint, or measuring windows. There was less scraping needed inside, so the women set to work washing the walls. As soon as they were dry, paint cans were opened, and ladies worked side by side brushing on fresh bright colors. It didn't matter what language they spoke, because they were communicating in the language of helpfulness and caring.

Mid-day, the women stopped painting and started preparing food. Baskets of bread and fruit were carried from the cars. The Mexican women rolled tortillas, heaped meat and cheese on them, folded and fried them, making hot *empanadillas*. Soon, they called everyone to come eat.

Tito carried his plate over toward Dana and sat down beside him. "I like your car, *Senõr* Dana. Could we take a ride sometime?"

"You're Tito, right?"

The boy nodded.

"I'll take you for a ride all by yourself, with the top down, if your mother says 'OK,'" Dana said. Then he bit into the warm, cheesy *empanadilla* and smiled.

## 22. TITO TRUSTS DANA

"You're the man of the day," Dana said to Tito as they pulled away from the building, which was quickly becoming gray where the green paint was brushed off.

"Do you think so, *Senõr*?" Tito asked.

"Hey, cut out the Seen-yor stuff. I'm just a kid like you. Maybe a bigger kid. But I'm not ready to be an adult. Call me Dana."

"I would like that. Your car is fast!" Tito exclaimed, as Dana accelerated quickly after they turned north on Centerline Road.

They went all the way into Cherry Hill and drove around several blocks. People waved at the happy boys in the cute yellow roaster, and Dana and Tito waved back.

As they were returning to Cherry Pit Junction, Tito said, "Can I ask you something important?"

"Sure thing," Dana answered, slowing the car so it was quieter and looking intently at the boy beside him.

"Your father, Mr. Bigg, is the man that owns the building where I live, right?"

"Yes, Mr. Harold L. Bigg. Technically, I'm Mr. Bigg too, Dana P. Bigg. But I don't like to be called that. It makes people think I'm like him."

"*Si*, that is what I want to talk to you about," Tito said slowly. "My own *Papá* did bad things, too. I do not want to become like him."

"You don't have to," Dana said.

"But maybe I can't help it. You are nice. Are you afraid sometimes you might be like your father?"

Dana hadn't expected such a thoughtful question from a small boy. Although he liked to act as if serious topics didn't interest him, deep down, he cared very much. His college studies so far had been general. He hadn't declared a major because his father wanted him to go into business, but what Dana wanted was to become a psychologist and help people. He kept putting off the decision that he knew would make his father unhappy.

"We do inherit some traits from our parents," Dana replied. "Of course, the way we look, or maybe a talent for sports or art. But we make our own choices about the kind of person we want to become."

"But, do you think about becoming like your father?" Tito persisted.

"Yes, Tito, I do. But he was not always so hard and mean. Before my mother died, he was much nicer."

"Your *mamá* is dead?" Tito exclaimed. "That is sad."

"She died six years ago of pneumonia. I miss her."

"What was her name?"

"Her name was Kathryn."

"*Mamá*'s full name is Rosa Leticia Teresa Gonzales Fernandez. Fernandez was her last name before she was married. But in this country people don't use long names or add the second family name. Here, she is just called Rosa."

"Like a nickname. My mother was called Kitty. She was a beautiful and loving woman." Dana sighed. "Always treasure your mother, Tito. Always."

"*Sí*, Dana. I will do that." But Tito's mind was racing. Could the lady who wrote the pink letters be a woman named Kathryn?"

\*\*\*

By the end of the day, a form for a concrete slab had been built along the entire front of the building, and a big truck with a rolling mixer drum arrived to fill it. As some of the men worked to level the concrete, Mr. Mosher explained to Rosa Gonzales, "We're adding a closed porch all along here. This will give everyone an entry space to hang field clothes and boots, and provide a common walkway to the toilets. That way, no one has to go all the way outside to reach the bathroom any more."

Ken appeared and slapped Jimmie's father, Jed Mosher, on the back. "That's the bee's knees! This slab will be set enough to build on by Monday."

"Let's hope the weather holds," Jed said. "Our work crew will be smaller when the work week starts for the businessmen. The farmers will stick with you, though. And the children will be available until Tuesday."

Cora, with Ruby by her side, stepped up to Ken. Her overalls were dusty with paint flakes and she had a streak of blue on her face and across one braid. It matched the brush in her hand and the new color of the building. "Are we doing a good job?" she asked. "This is fun, and I feel like I'm really being useful."

"It's hard work, but I can paint the bottom rows without a ladder," Ruby said.

"You are a great help, kids," Ken said. "We couldn't do it without you."

"We finished that end," Laszlo said, coming around the corner with some of the Mexican boys.

The sun was falling toward the horizon. "Let's wash the brushes and knock off for today," Ken suggested.

"We'll be back after church tomorrow," Jed said. There were smiles on every face, and plenty of hugs were passed around.

## 23. MR. BIGG FINDS OUT

The next day was a lot like Saturday. The painting continued, and the older children were allowed to go on the roof and begin stripping off the old shingles.

"We'll cut a hole up there for a stovepipe," Ken explained, pointing to the roof above the Gonzales' apartment.

"*Gracias*. We will have heat this winter," Rosa said, touching Ken's arm.

"Simply a wood stove and only in this one apartment," Ken answered.

"That is enough. We know how to use it safely, and we are the only family that is staying all year."

"Tomorrow, refrigerators and new stoves will be delivered for each unit," Dana said. "Everyone needs good appliances. Martin Harris is repairing the electric wiring today."

Dana heard the distant roar of a powerful engine and looked up.

Cora and Jimmie were on the roof, hauling an armload of old shingles toward the edge where they could throw them into the back of the Szep's pickup truck. Jimmie glanced north, up Centerline Road, and saw a large black car approaching. "Hey, that's a Chrysler Imperial," he said. "You don't see many of them out here. It's a new one, too. I'll bet it has air conditioning and disc brakes."

Jimmie was shocked when the huge chrome-laden vehicle pulled off the road and stopped practically beneath him. A man wearing a blue suit with a captain's hat emerged from the driver's seat. He opened the rear door.

Mr. Harold L. Bigg himself stepped out. He pulled down his suit coat and straightened his tie, wiggling his large head from side to side and grimacing. He took a deep breath. "Dana Perham Bigg!" he called in such a commanding tone that everyone stopped working to look at him.

Most of the people there did not know who the man was, so they were only curious as to what was going to happen next.

The children who had met him, in his office, felt a little frightened. They remembered that he'd threatened to charge anyone who tried to fix the building with a crime.

Dana was not entirely surprised to see his father. He was annoyed that he'd been called out like a small child, but he was prepared to defend his actions in repairing the living quarters for the factory workers.

Tito had the strangest reaction of all. He didn't seem to be paying any attention to the large man with the big voice. He ran inside his house and lifted the corner of his mattress. At first he wondered if he'd heard Mr. Bigg correctly. Then he wondered if he'd read the letters correctly. He pulled out the pink pages and checked the one signed with a full name. "Kitty Perham." There it was. It couldn't be a coincidence that Dana's middle name was Perham and his mother's name was Kitty. His own mother's name included her maiden name. Maybe Americans did that sometimes too.

He re-read one of the letters. Could Harold Bigg be Harry? He wasn't sure, but certainly the letters belonged to Dana. Tito didn't hesitate, or think for even a second about asking Dana for money to get the letters back. He knew the right thing to do, and he did it. Taking the six envelopes, he went outside, blinking in the sunlight.

Dana and his father were having an argument. They'd stepped to the other side of the road and lowered their voices. Tito could see from their faces and actions that they were both upset. But he couldn't wait.

He crossed the road and pulled on Dana's arm. "Please, *Senõr*... Dana."

"Not now, Tito," Dana said.

"But, this is important. These, I think, are yours." He thrust the letters into Dana's hand and stepped back. He started to return to his house.

Dana was about to stick the papers in a pocket, but then he looked down and saw the handwriting. His father kept talking, but Dana began reading. Once he started, he couldn't stop.

Harold Bigg just kept ranting, thinking he was getting the upper hand since his son was quiet.

"Dad, stop," Dana commanded.

Something in his son's tone made the man close his mouth and look at the boy.

\*\*\*

From across the road, everyone had now stopped working and was watching this strange scene. Word had quickly spread that Mr. Bigg was the owner who had not wanted to repair the housing, so they desperately wanted young Dana Bigg to win the argument.

It was hard to imagine what Tito could have given Dana that was causing such a change in what was happening. They watched the son hand some pink papers to his father. Mr. Bigg's face went white and he sat down on the rusty guardrail, apparently without any concern for his expensive suit. The man pulled out a silver penknife and slit several envelopes, reading page after page. When he had finished, he just sat there quietly. Finally, he pulled a handkerchief from a pocket and wiped his forehead. Some people said they saw him wipe his eyes as well.

## 24. THE TALE OF KITTY AND HARRY

Mr. Bigg and Dana came across the road.

"Can someone find my father a chair?" Dana said. "He's had a shock."

A chair was brought outside, and Mr. Bigg sat down. "Where is the young man who had these letters?" he asked.

Now Tito was frightened. Mr. Bigg was an important man and it was always the brown-skinned people who got in trouble. He cowered beside his mother.

"Come here, Tito," Dana said, holding out his hand. "You've done nothing wrong."

Tito stepped forward slowly.

"Where did you get these letters," Mr. Bigg asked, waving the pink pages and envelopes in the air.

"I found them in the kitchen. There..." Tito said, pointing vaguely in the direction of his rooms. "They were behind the wooden shelves. I gave them back as soon as I figured out the Kitty lady must be Dana's mother."

Rosa Gonzales began to scold Tito in rapid Spanish.

"Don't be angry with the boy," Harold Bigg said. "Let me tell you a story."

Men and women nodded and smiled. They liked stories. More chairs were produced, and some people sat on the ground.

"A long time ago, when I was Dana's age, I was in love with a young girl named Kathryn, or Kitty, Perham. She called me Harry. Our fathers were business associates. But when the banks failed in 1929 her father lost everything. They had to go on the road doing hard work, like many families during those times. My father had different investments and wasn't financially hurt as badly."

"This is what I asked you about," Tito said, looking up at his mother.

Rosa put an arm around her oldest son and nodded.

Reeta Dubois sucked in a lungful of air. "*The Grapes of Wrath*," she said.

"Yes, very much like in that book," Mr. Bigg said. "Anyway, Kitty and her family seemingly disappeared. I searched and asked around, and I finally found them right here."

"And you saved her!" Ruby exclaimed.

"No, young lady, it wasn't that simple. Her father wouldn't let me anywhere near her. He accused me of being a nuisance and got the police to tell me to stay away. Meanwhile, I never heard a thing from the girl I loved."

"But what about the letters?" Cora asked.

"She never got to mail them," Tito said. He suddenly felt bashful for telling the story that wasn't his. "It was in the letters," he explained.

"That's exactly right," Mr. Bigg continued. "Her father became more and more controlling. He locked her up here. He finally had a nervous breakdown. When Kitty got away and came to me, she had made up a story about being on vacation in Europe. I knew it wasn't true, but I didn't want to embarrass her. I let her think I believed that."

"These are letters my mother wrote to my father when she lived in the very same apartment as Tito," Dana said. "He found them and has returned them to us. Thanks, Tito, this means a lot, now that Mother is dead."

There was a collective sigh of sympathy and some whispering.

"You five friends, come here," Mr. Bigg ordered. "And Tito, too."

Jimmie, Cora, Laszlo, George, Ruby, and Tito stepped forward. Mr. Bigg motioned them closer.

"I was very cross with you, and I want to apologize. This building holds a lot of unhappy memories for me, which had a strong grip on me. But I think Kitty would want me to let go of them. It's as if she has spoken to me from beyond the grave. And you five were brave enough to challenge me to think about my actions."

"And we'll finish the repairs," Dana said.

"We'll do more than that," Mr. Bigg said. He was not one to let another person have the better idea, even his own son. "As soon as the factory shuts down for the winter, in two weeks, I'll tear this place down and put up a decent apartment building. I'll rent a house in town for the Gonzales family while it's being built."

There was applause and a few cheers.

"Tito, come here and shake my hand!" Mr. Bigg ordered.

Tito stepped forward and extended his small hand. It was grasped in Mr.Bigg's large one. He felt respected.

"This is a fine, honest boy you have, Mrs. Gonzales. Hopefully, his father, Juan, will take a lesson from the son. I'll give him another chance as soon as he's served his jail term."

Tito glowed with the praise, and decided he was beginning to understand how to make good choices for his life.

# PAPER DOLLS

Trace the boy and girl doll separately and cut them out of cardboard or stiff paper. Color the hair and skin to match you or your friends, or maybe even someone you don't know. Cut out the doll.

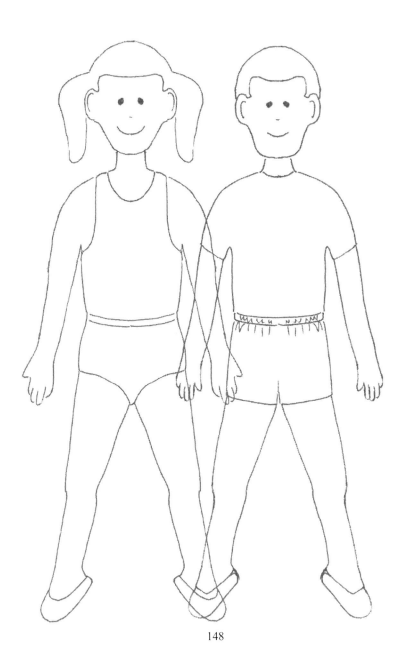

Follow the edges of the dolls on another sheet of plain paper to make clothes that fit, and then add tabs to hold them in place. Color and cut out the clothes you made and put them on the doll.

**tabs**

**tabs**

# CURSIVE WRITING

This is a chart of the Palmer Method Cursive alphabet. If you practice copying this a few times you'll easily get the hang of it. Connect all the letters in a word to each other. If the word begins with a capital letter it might not connect to the rest of the word. Only a few letters are very different from printing. These are capitals A, G, I, J, Q, S and Z, and lower case f, r, s, and z.

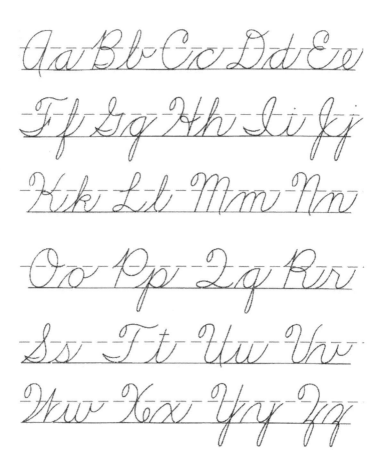

My name is:                          What's yours?

# ACKNOWLEDGEMENTS

A huge statement of thanks and artistic credit goes to my good friend and partner in fun, Ester Lamb. The beginnings of this story grew naturally from what might have happened when the children returned to school in September after capturing the ring of thieves in *The ABZ Affair*. However, I was having trouble imagining an ending for the book which kept the children involved in solutions. She instantly saw Dana Bigg as a person who would reach out to the children to help, and keep them in the story.

Also, perhaps even more critically, she invented the sub-plot of Kitty's family's financial ruin, and the letters which provided a strong enough motive for Mr. Bigg to change his ways. This story really flies because of Ester, who claims it was an incredible pleasure to help build the tale.

I also owe a large debt to my friends Chuck and Sylvia Hutchinson who spent many years among Central American Spanish-speaking people. They kept my Spanish on track, and provided cultural advice.

As always, any final errors are the fault of the author.

Joan H. Young, July 2018

# OTHER PUBLISHED WORKS
# BY JOAN H. YOUNG

## Non-Fiction:

North Country Cache: Adventures on a National Scenic Trail

Would You Dare?

Devotions for Hikers

## Fiction:

### Anastasia Raven Mysteries:

News from Dead Mule Swamp

The Hollow Tree at Dead Mule Swamp

Paddy Plays in Dead Mule Swamp

Bury the Hatchet in Dead Mule Swamp

Dead Mule Swamp Druggist

### The Dubois Files:

listed at the front of this volume

# ABOUT THE AUTHOR

 Joan H. Young has enjoyed the out-of-doors her entire life. Highlights of her outdoor adventures include Girl Scouting, which provided yearly training in camp skills, the opportunity to engage in a ten-day canoe trip, and numerous short backpacking excursions. She was selected to attend the 1965 Senior Scout Roundup in Coeur d'Alene, Idaho, an international event to which 10,000 girls were invited. She rode a bicycle from the Pacific to the Atlantic Ocean in 1986, and on August 3, 2010 became the first woman to complete the North Country National Scenic Trail on foot. Her mileage totaled 4395 miles. She often writes and gives media programs about her outdoor experiences.

In 2010 she began writing more fiction, including several award-winning short stories. The Bigg Boss is the fourth book in the Dubois Files mystery series.

Visit booksleavingfootprints.com for more information.